The Painter's Women

Goya in Light and Shade

a novel

FIONNUALA BRENNAN

Fionnuala Brennan

BETIMES BOOKS

First published in the English language worldwide in 2015
by Betimes Books

ISBN 978-0-9929674-8-2

Cover design by JT Lindroos

ALSO BY FIONNUALA BRENNAN

FICTION:

ALL THINGS RETURN

NON-FICTION:

ON A GREEK ISLAND

For our two lovely
daughters, Orla and Fiona,
the most important women
in my life.

"For my part, I see only forms that are lit up and forms that are not. There is only light and shade."

—Francisco de Goya

1

ROSARIO
BORDEAUX, 16 APRIL, 1828

Energeia. That's the Greek word for action. Energy is life. A man might as well be dead if he does not live energetically. My father's eyes sparked when he used to say that and his broad, paint-spattered hands encompassed the world. For that is how Papa lived and now he is dead.

None of the others know that I am here beside him. I could not leave him all alone until morning. How could I sleep, thinking of him abandoned on these ghostly pillows, his fierce eyes weighted with coins, his querulous mouth clamped shut?

They are all sleeping, even Mama. I crept back to be with him after they had left – Mama, Gumersinda, Mariano, that painter fellow, Antonio Brugada, and the others who came and stood in a circle around his bed last night, like disciples waiting to hear a prophecy. Papa did not open his eyes; he just lay there grunting and mumbling to himself, as was his custom. Told them nothing; gave them no last message. What was there to say, after all? Everything they need to know he has already told them. Why do they not *look* at his work?

As the moon was growing smaller in the sky, at two o'clock this morning my Papa gave up his struggle. He left this life when he felt his great energy leaving him. So it is over. No breath lifts his great chest beneath the sheet. No matter how hard I strain to catch the slightest sound, there is nothing. It is as if a waterfall, which has thundered and poured over me through my life, suddenly reduces to a trickle and stops. I cannot believe that he has gone from me.

Oh Papa, wake up! Please don't leave me. I cannot bear to be without you. It's not fair. We *need* you, Mama and I. You *said* you would live to be as old as Titian. Santa Maria, what will become of us?

Oh, it's no good my calling him. He *is* dead. My dearest Papa, who saw himself as Colossus straddling the world. If he had not worked so hard making those lithographs day and night, if only he had listened to his doctors, if he had paid any heed to Mama, maybe he would still be alive, even if he was eighty-two years of age. Nobody as old as he was should work as he did – like a madman. Papa always did exactly as he pleased, no matter what anyone said. And now he has left me in the dark, he who was the light of my life.

What a selfish girl I am! Papa is barely three hours dead, and I am concerned only about myself. Wait! What was that? Listen! Was that not a low, shallow breath? Surely the sheet is lifting, just a little, above his chest? I knew it! Such a powerful person as Papa could not be snuffed out like a candle. God is merciful. Papa lives. *Santissima*, a miracle! We are saved, Mama and me. Let me kiss your face, Papa.

Delirious girl. Fool. His forehead is as cold as altar marble, no breath stirs the sheet. He was a very old man who had been deathly ill for weeks. Paralysed. Finished this time.

Not like at La Quinta. There's no Doctor Arrieta to save him here in Bordeaux.

I think souls must linger around this world before they go to Heaven or Hell, or wherever they go. They must stay with the living for some time after they die, because I can *feel* Papa's energy still. It fills this room like a crowd. It's as if his body is lying lifeless on the bed, but his *self* is everywhere, like... a veil, yes, like a veil or a mist floating over the room, touching the walls, the ceiling, the cabinet, brushing against the backs of the chairs, *breathing*. So we are still together, Papa, and I can talk to you for a little while longer. And you'll be able to hear as you used to before you became deaf, because you are a spirit now and perfect.

I would like to know, Papa, what is dying like? Is it all blackness, as in a tunnel? Like falling into an abyss? Were you very afraid? I can't imagine that you were. Or were you simply too tired to care whether you lived or died? Perhaps you were glad to go finally. For how could you go on living when you had lost your strength? *A man might as well be dead if he does not live energetically.* If you could no longer paint or make lithographs, that would have been worse than death for you. May you rest in peace, Papa.

But could someone like you ever be at peace? Could such a man as you find rest in Heaven? Would you not stir up things there as you did on earth? Trouble seemed to follow you all your life. We had to flee from La Quinta because of some danger you said was threatening you. And then there were all those problems you had with the Holy Office, which Mama told me about, when King Ferdinand returned to rule in Spain. She said you were forced to appear before the Inquisition. I don't know why. Nobody tells me anything properly. I am fourteen years old, no longer a silly little girl, and they should all realise that.

Oh, Papa, I can't think clearly. Everything that was certain in my life is gone. I feel lost. I sense another feeling too. Something hot in my chest. Forgive me, but I'm angry with you Papa. You've deserted me. And I'm angry with God for taking you from me and with Javier and his family for being so horrible to me. Angry too with myself, for being so selfish. It's sinful of me to feel like this at such a time but, Papa, I can't control what feelings rise up in me, can I? And I shall say exactly what I feel. You did. And you also *did* exactly what you wanted to, no matter what anyone else thought. That's why we are living here in Bordeaux, and not at La Quinta. That's why... ah, that's why so many things. Things I only half-hear about, things whispered in the kitchen by the maids, things Mama brushes aside when I ask questions.

We have some time to be together before the dawn, before they all come back and claim you for themselves. You are mine for a little while longer, Papa.

Let's go back to La Quinta, shall we? We were so happy there, weren't we? So let's go there once more. You're covering the walls of the house with enormous pictures, painted for yourself, you said, and not for any patron. I remember that when we went there first you painted lovely landscapes on those walls; with big, wide skies filled with sun, and trees – you loved trees; people laughing and dancing, full of life. I liked looking at those pictures. But soon afterwards you painted over them. Giant black paintings. When I asked you a few months ago why you had destroyed the lovely landscapes with those dark pictures, you said it was because Spain was in turmoil then, that cruelty, superstition and folly ruled the country and so you could not paint light in such darkness.

You shouted a lot while you were painting. Mama was afraid to go near you when you were working, but in the evenings, after you had finished for the day, you were calm. As if the painting and the shouting had got rid of something that was troubling you.

That giant, it must be you! You, Don Francisco de Goya, with the unruly, black, springy hair you must have had when you were younger, your fiery staring eyes, your person, gigantic and angry, dominating the chaotic world far below you, shaking your massive fist at it, and cursing the cruelty and the chaos. What an angry man you were sometimes, Papa. But only in your paintings, and with Mama sometimes; never with me.

We're playing at bullfighting. You're the bull, as usual, and today I'm Costilliares, because he was your favourite *torero*. Mama's red shawl is my *muleta* and your walking cane is my sword. You're coming towards me, snorting, your fingers sticking up at each side your head and your feet pawing the ground. I swirl my *muleta* and sidestep your horns. Swish, swish! You charge past me and skid to a halt, turn and charge again. I look you in the eye and raise my sword, but I lower it again and say, 'I will spare your life. For you are a good old bull and I love you.' Then we race to the fountain, and the famous *torero* and the bull splash each other and laugh and laugh.

After the bullfight we go inside, you to your dark paintings and me to continue the chocolate hunt. I run all over the house, searching in every room. Under the beds, among your tubs of paint, in all the closets, in every bowl in the kitchen. Got it! Behind the green water pitcher in the kitchen. A great big slab of chocolate, not yet melted, so you must have hidden it not long before. I hear you laughing behind the door. *Papa, thank you, thank you.* There is chocolate all over my face and splotches of it on my good white dress and Mama is screaming, *You are spoiling that child, Francisco. And look at the state of that dress!*

I run into the garden then where Mama can't see me. You come out, too, carrying your drawing things. When Mama screams, you often just walk out of the house. I poke under the bushes with a stick, climb a ladder into the fig tree and look in all the little holes between the branches, lifting the leaves. Here it is! Cunningly wrapped in green paper and tied underneath a big leaf. What is inside? A spinning top, red and blue. You're sitting in your chair drawing, pretending not to see me. 'Look at what I found, Papa. Hidden under a leaf.'

'Goodness. A spinning top under a leaf! I wonder who could have put it here. A hobgoblin do you think?'

'Mysterious Papa. It was you!'

'Don't tell your mother where you got it. She would not like to hear you've been climbing trees, would she?'

Sometimes it was combs, at other times satin ribbons – which you must have bought yourself, because Mama was always surprised when she saw me wearing them.

Another day. It's a hot summer afternoon. I'm sitting as quiet as a mouse on my little chair watching you high up on a ladder, painting the wall in the salon. You are painting a woman you call Judith.

'Who is Judith, Papa?'

'Child, go and read your Bible and you will find out.'

'But, Papa, I am only six and cannot read.'

'Then I'll tell the Judith story to you at bedtime tonight.'

But you did not read me any story that night, because suddenly, without a cry, you fell off the ladder, as if you had fainted and lost your balance, and by the time I ran over to you, you were lying on your back like a beetle, so still.

'Mama, come. Come quickly. Papa's dead!'

Mama and Joaquina came running into the room. They dragged you to your bed and sent Carlos to fetch Doctor Arrieta. He came at full speed on his panting horse and dashed into your bedroom, his big leather bag slung over his shoulder.

For long days I was not allowed to see you. Mama and the servants crept around the house, talking in whispers. *Santa Maria, save my Papa.* I lit candles and put flowers in front of the image of the Virgin. The doctor came every day for a week and stayed for hours at your bedside. After that, I was allowed in to see my Papa again. I will never forget that day.

You were propped up against the pillows, wearing a heavy dressing gown buttoned over your chest, although the weather was very hot. How old you had become – an old, old man. You could hardly open your eyes and your mouth was hanging open like a fish. Your hands were clutching the red bedcover as if you were drowning.

'Mariquita,' you whispered at last. 'Do not worry, little one; your father is not ready to die just yet.'

I could not see your eyes and your face was as yellow as old cheese, but a little smile hovered around your mouth. So I did not worry.

How I loved you saying your pet name for me, *Mariquita.*

Next thing, off you go again, living energetically. Back at your easel, painting a picture of the good doctor, which you gave to him as a present for saving your life. Oh, if only Doctor Arrieta were here in Bordeaux, he would have saved you. But what's the use of wishing now? I could waste my whole life wishing.

Back to La Quinta again. After you finish the portrait of Doctor Arrieta, you start another big painting on the wall of the salon; a monster, you called Saturn, eating a human head. Judith is on one side of the door and Saturn is on the other.

'Is Saturn in the Bible, too, Papa?'

'Do you not know any mythology, child?'

'What's mythology, Papa?'

'I forget that you're only six, Rosario. I'll tell you about Saturn when you are a little older. It's a frightening story.'

That's you, the old man leaning on a stick on the other side of the room, isn't it? I'm sure that figure is you because someone is shouting into his ear. I love watching you work. The black monsters don't frighten me one bit. They're like fairy stories, but for grown-ups.

But all the days at La Quinta were not happy. Especially at the end, not long before we had to flee. One day was really unhappy for me.

Mariano and his father, Javier, have come out from Madrid to visit you. Certainly not to see Mama or me. *To squeeze some more money or property out of the old man, more likely,* Mama is muttering to herself. I'm nine years old. I see you walking under the orange trees. Your arm is resting on Mariano's shoulder. He's a tall young fellow of seventeen. I'm running towards you calling, 'Papa, Papa, I've found the chocolate surprise!' You stoop down, pick me up, and swing me round and round until I'm dizzy. Then you put me gently on the ground again, and kiss the top of my head. I look up and see Mariano's face. It's like a thundercloud. I'm frightened. He looks at me as if I'm an insect. Then he strides away from us as fast as he can. You don't seem to notice. I take your hand and squeeze it hard. You squeeze mine and smile.

Then you go back indoors to your painting. Mariano comes to find me in the garden.

'Let's play hide and seek,' he says.

I'm surprised because he never plays with me, but I run off and hide in one of the storehouses farthest from the house. I'm crouching behind some sacks of potatoes when I hear his footsteps outside. I hold my breath. He opens the door, but doesn't come in.

'I know you're in there, *bastarda*,' he shouts, and I hear the key being turned in the lock.

Bastarda? What does he mean? It's dark and there's a smell of must from the sacks and the scratching sound of mice. I run towards the door.

'Mariano, Mariano, you found me! Now it's your turn to hide, and I'll look for you.'

But the door is locked, and Mariano is laughing in a strange way.

'Let me out please, Mariano.'

A long time passes. I plead and cry. The scrabbling sound of the mice grows louder and I begin to see strange shapes hovering over the sacks and barrows. The rakes begin to move and the spades shift menacingly along the walls. Still Mariano says nothing, but I know he's outside. He is smoking a cigar; I can smell the smoke coming under the door.

Finally I scream: 'You have to let me out. I'll tell Papa what you've done. He'll be angry with you.'

'He's not your Papa, little bastard. Never dare to call my grandfather *Papa* again, you hear?'

'But what should I call him? He *is* my Papa. He *is*, he *is*.' I feel feverish.

'No, he's not. Your mother is a servant in this house. She is not my grandfather's wife; therefore you are not his daughter.'

He kept me locked in that dark smelly place for hours, it seemed, and only when I promised never again to call my father *Papa* did he let me out. God forgive him, for I cannot. I know he's your beloved grandson, Papa, but he's my enemy. I don't know why he hates me so much. I don't know, either, why Javier and Gumersinda despise my Mama and me. We have never done anything bad to them. We have not taken you away from them. Indeed, we have looked after you well, haven't we?

'I should like you to look at her as if she were my daughter and I shall repay you,' I heard you telling your friend Don Joaquin Ferrer.

I was so pleased when I heard you saying that. But I am *not* so pleased when I recall it now. I'm sorry, Papa, but *why* could you not have omitted that phrase, 'as if she were'? I *am* your daughter. Perhaps you weren't so fearless after all, or as unconventional as you prided yourself on being. Oh, forgive me, Papa, for blaming you, for thinking only of myself again.

Oh, you could open those heavy eyelids of yours right now, and glower at the world once more. You could suddenly fling away that heavy black crucifix they have stuck between your hands! And you could push out your thick bottom lip, tilt that obstinate chin, and make one of your outrageous statements. Like one of those wild-looking prophets in the Bible.

But first of all, you would smile at me, and call me your little Mariquita. To think I shall never be called that name again. Or watch you at work, or help you set up your easel, or prepare the stone for lithographs, or listen to your stories about all the important people you used to know in Spain. There is only Mama to love me now.

Are you happy, Papa, that your long, hard life is over? Happy that you will not have to witness any more stupidities of people, or vanities, as you used to call them, nor endure more wars, cruelties and hypocrisy? Happy that you do not have to worry about being dragged before the Inquisition, or driven into exile, or being watched by the King's spies? Or are you sad because, despite having struggled so hard to recover from your other serious illnesses, this time you did not win? Are you disappointed to discover you could not cheat death once more? Are you furious with yourself because you can no longer lift a brush or a pencil to stab at what you called the folly of this world?

Even a week ago, when it was clear to all of us that you could not postpone death much longer, you were calling to me to fetch your pencils, and bellowing like a bleeding bull because you could not hold a pencil or see to draw. And Mama was crying and hushing you, urging you not to exhaust yourself. The look you gave her! The word *exhaust* had no meaning for you.

'Get out,' you rasped, your voice hoarse with frustration. 'All of you except Rosario.'

After they had left – Mama looking stricken, like a child who had been spanked for something she had not done – you asked me to come closer. Made me sit right here, beside your face, asked me to bend down to hear your suddenly weakened voice.

'Promise me one thing, child,' you said.

Your eyes were wild like storms. Your fingers were imprisoning mine, not like a beggar, not pleading, but like chains.

'Promise that you will always paint what comes from your own imagination, not servile imitations. Paint your own invention, never what is fashionable. Nothing that is expected. Promise me that. Promise.'

I nodded and stroked your powerful fist.

'For one day you will be a great painter, my daughter,' you went on, your voice urgent. 'Your old father knows it. Do not dishonour me, Mariquita. Always make art from your own imagination. Let your patrons make of it what they will. There will be some who will understand. The rest do not matter. In any case, you'll have enough money to live independently. I've seen to that. I've instructed Javier to look after your mother and you very well indeed. So promise me you will always be independent as an artist. Do not allow the demands of a husband, or children, or domestic cares, to prevent your promise being fulfilled. You must not! Swear to me that nobody will dictate the art you will make. And when the day comes when you know you are good enough, then use my name. But not until then. Do you understand?'

That was not the first time, Papa, that you had told me you had arranged for Mama and me to be taken care of. Before we had to flee from La Quinta, you took me on your knee, and you held my face in your big hands and said, 'Little one, your Papa will look after you. Please do not be afraid. You and your Mama will always have money enough for your needs and a place to live.'

That was the same day that Mariano and Javier had come to visit you. As they were driving away in their splendid carriage, I remember both of them looking very pleased with themselves. Mariano turned back as the horses went out through the gates and shouted at me: 'You've lost, little girl. And we've won.' I've often wondered what he meant by that.

What will we do, Mama and I, now that you've left us? Where will we go? I know, I know, it's petty and selfish of me to keep thinking such thoughts, but I feel as if a great protecting rock has been rolled away, leaving me and Mama exposed like two scuttling insects. Mama would be angry with me if she knew I'm comparing her to a scuttling insect, and she would be justified, for she isn't in the least weak in her nature. You always said that she was too strong-willed for a woman. What I mean is that our position in this family is weak without you to stand up for us. How will Javier and Mariano and Gumersinda treat us now? Pray God you have kept your word to me, and provided for us as you promised.

Yes, yes. I am quite certain that you have. You wouldn't let us down. Why should I doubt my father? Didn't you love me just as much as you loved Javier? You often said so. Therefore, I shouldn't trouble myself about what will happen to Mama and me. Why should you have made such promises otherwise? And why indeed should you not provide for your only daughter and for your second wife? For that is what Mama is, even if it is not a normal marriage, and if, for that reason, both of us are somehow unofficial Goyas.

Now I feel your spirit, or your self, or your energy, fading. It's rising like a mist. It's leaving the room. It's gone! Oh, this is too hard to bear. It's not fair. My friend Carmen's papa is alive and strong. And all my other friends' fathers are well. Why shouldn't I have a papa too? I want him back...

It's so quiet in here. I daren't move lest I disturb the air around him. My feet are as heavy as clay, and numb. My chest aches with crying and my eyes are stinging like nettles. This is the longest night. Yet I do not want it to end.

If only he could have stayed a while longer. Just till morning. What will I do when they take him away in a casket, and close the lid, and put him in a tomb, and I'll never see him again?

A moth is circling the candles around the bed; its shadow on the wall is a dark beast, like a monster in his paintings. What a heartless girl I am, noticing the shadow of a moth when my father lies dead. But Papa used to say that an artist never stops observing. And I *am* going to be the artist he wants me to become.

Francisco – he was raving about someone called Francisco yesterday. I wonder who that was. *El Pilar*, where is that place? Yesterday – what an age ago that seems – I was alone with him. (Everyone else had gone to eat but I couldn't leave him.) His eyes were closed, his breathing laboured, and he hadn't spoken for hours, so that I thought he was unconscious. Suddenly his eyelids flew open and he started muttering feverishly, his big hands wringing the bedclothes.

'Francisco,' he gasped, and his whole body was moving like a snake under the covers. 'Francisco! El Pilar. A mistake. A great mistake.'

My father, the great Goya, actually said the word 'mistake.' If he meant *his* mistake, then surely the approach of death changes people profoundly. Of course, he might have meant that this other Francisco fellow was to blame. But all that writhing? Papa must have felt very bad about that mistake, whatever it was.

Then other names; 'Pepa, my dear faithful Pepa.' I know who that was: his first wife, Doña Josefa. Mama told me that she had died quite a long time ago. Before Mama came to live with him. Before I was born.

But who is *Cayetana*? He smiled when he said that name and raised his right hand and stared at a ring on his third finger. I cannot remember all the names he called out; there were such a lot of them. *Good Martin*, I remember that, because that is Don Martin Zapater, the man to whom he had me write a letter only a week ago.

'Martin Zapater is my oldest friend,' he said. 'We've known each other since we were at Father Joaquin's school in Fuendetodos together. We've been writing to each other all our lives. He's the only one who really knows your father.'

When I asked Mama to post the letter, she was angry.

'Has that foolish old man forgotten that Don Martin died years ago?' she snapped.

Mama is quite unfair sometimes. Perhaps she doesn't like it that Papa said Don Martin was the only one who really knew him.

He went on like that for a long while, calling out names, as if he was reading out a list he saw in front of him. Papa knew such a great number of people: kings and queens, dukes and duchesses, poets, writers. And when he talked about them, he did not seem in the least in awe of their high status.

'I may have been born the son of a humble gilder,' he once told me, 'but a great artist is superior to any grandee. Many of them pass their days puffing themselves up like peacocks in their palaces, twittering nonsense, and vying with each other in following the latest fashion in dress or conversation. There are a few, it has to be admitted, who are intelligent, who are sensitive, and who attempt to do something for their people. But *we*, the artists – only we can mirror people to themselves. In our creations, we explain the world. We show the contradictions and the riddles at the heart of it. Never forget that, my child.'

How I loved it when he called me 'my child' or 'my daughter.' But he never did it when Mariano, Javier or

Gumersinda were with us. I don't know if Papa knew that they had forbidden me to call my own father *Papa*. Once when I forgot, Doña Gumersinda flew into such a rage, stamping her foot, screaming at me never to dare to use that name again, shouting that Mama and I should never have been given shelter. Then she swept out of the room, roaring to Mariano and Javier that they all had to leave *at once*.

'Housekeeper,' she hissed at Mama, 'teach your brat to mind her manners and to stop telling such shameful lies.'

Papa's back was turned at the time, and so he didn't witness her tirade, but if he had known, what would his reaction have been, I wonder? Would he have claimed me? Although he always seemed so sure of himself, and would argue with anyone, I believe he was always a little afraid of his son. He indulged him, gave him a grand house, and so much money, everything he desired. Mama says Papa would do nothing to displease Javier, or his wife.

Even though Mama is some sort of relative of her family, the Goicoecheas, Gumersinda seems to think that she is of no consequence. As for Mariano, he treats me like a servant. Not in front of Papa, of course; he's too clever for that. I could never say all these things to Papa. I didn't wish to hurt him, or to cause any conflict, but now I have to think about them, even if it upsets me.

I'm not allowed to use my own father's name, and must be called Weiss (like my brother who really is a Weiss.) Mama says that's because and she and Papa are not married in the usual way, and that the world is a strange place in which a woman's children are always considered to be her legal husband's, whether that's true or not. I've never even *seen* Señor Isidoro Weiss, whom they say is my legal father, and I never want to meet him. For what is he to me? Nothing. He's simply a man to whom my mother was married once upon a time. Before she went to look after Papa, before they took me to La Quinta del Sordo.

That's where I belong and that is exactly where I want to return. Although Papa often said that I speak French like a native, and I've made friends here in Bordeaux, I miss my own country, and especially La Quinta. Four years is quite long enough in France. I'm going to insist that after Papa is buried we return to Spain.

We can live at La Quinta again. I'll walk through his rooms and look at his special paintings, really *look*, just as he did every day. Now that I'm older, and have studied art a little, I might be able to understand them better. At least I shall know which figures come from the Bible and which from mythology.

I thought our life at La Quinta would last forever. I believed Papa would go on painting until all the walls were covered, and then he would build more rooms and paint those too. I thought he would continue the grand extension of the garden which he had begun, ordering new plants and getting the gardener to put in trees wherever there was a space along the perimeter of our land. I expected that he and Mama would joke together, and sometimes argue too, and that he would play at bullfighting with me, and hide surprises for me all over the house and garden. I love La Quinta, the gardens he made there, even the black paintings on the walls... everything.

My goodness, how he and Mama argued and screamed at each other during those last days at La Quinta. It made me miserable to hear them.

'Why you fight so often with Papa?' I asked her. 'And why do you sometimes say that you regret wasting your youth and beauty on him? Don't you love him?'

She looked shocked. I thought she was going to spank me for my impertinence, but she stared out the window for a while and then answered: 'I love your Papa dearly, even though he's as old as my father, and deaf and sometimes very difficult to live with. I love him because he's a great artist and such great artists are not like ordinary mortals. It doesn't matter how old they are. Time is different where they are concerned. We live in the light of their genius; we glow in the brightness of their vision.'

Mama does go on at times! I do believe that she was in awe of Papa, though she would never admit it.

How I wept when I came into this room last night and watched him struggling until the very end. I bawled when his great gnarled hands finally lay motionless on the white sheet like the roots of a small tree. And when I saw Mama place the silver coins on his eyelids, and close his stubborn mouth, I thought my heart would burst.

But now, after hours sitting here in the black shadows looking at my Papa, I've stopped crying. And another feeling – I have to admit it – has risen in me. It's a strange feeling of lightness. Yes, that's the truth. May God forgive me for feeling like this. The truth is I am almost relieved that he's gone. He taught me to be honest, didn't he? I'm glad that he died quite quickly and that he died as sane as he ever was. I'm happy that right up to the last weeks he was drawing and painting, and making his miniatures on ivory and his lithographs with all his tremendous energy and passion.

Papa had three great passions; painting, hunting and bullfighting. I love those lithographs of the *corrida* that he published a few years ago. He told me that once he signed himself Francisco de los Toros. We often went to the arena in

Bordeaux together and he made sketches for those prints. How fast he worked! His pencil flying over the page, his eyes taking in everything around us. It was fascinating to watch him work. Such intense concentration! It was like being beside a great bright light which burned with tremendous heat. Now, I'm thinking of those other bullfighting prints, the *Tauromaquia* etchings that he made when I was about four, before we went to live at La Quinta, they are so exciting, especially the one of Martincho in the arena at Saragossa. Papa said Martincho was a famous torero who was so brave that he sat on a chair with his feet tied and faced the charging bull with his sword ready for the last thrust. He certainly was brave. Imagine, his feet tied!

The Milkmaid of Bordeaux, that's what Papa called his last painting. He worked on it for the last two years. How tenderly he painted me. And although he expended so much time and effort, it looks loosely done and easily achieved. It makes me happy that one of his last works is gentle and soft. He gave it to Mama and made her promise not to sell it for less than an ounce of gold. An ounce! Papa knew his worth.

It is getting light. Even from behind the heavy drapes, daylight is seeping in. Our time together, Papa, is over, so I must say my last goodbye. I don't know how we shall face the world without you. I'm so frightened. I love you so much, Papa. Look down from Heaven on me, now and ever after. Please look after your Mariquita from up there.

Papa, I'm dreading your funeral. Gumersinda and Mariano will expect to sit by themselves at the front of the church. Because you seemed to be sleeping or unconscious these past few days, maybe you did not realise that your beloved Javier, your Javier, your only son, did not bother to come here to see you before you died. Imagine! He still has not come. Gumersinda said he has some business to attend to in Madrid. What business could be more important than his dying father? I would never have treated you like that.

I fear that he and Gumersinda and Mariano will insist that *they* are the principal mourners in the church; that *they* are your only family. And where in the congregation will Mama and I be placed? Will we be expected to be squeezed at the back with the servants? Me, Rosario, your adopted and natural daughter. Mama, the one who looked after you like a wife all these years. I will *not* stand at the back. I will sit right up beside the rest of them. And Mama will sit beside me. You would wish that, wouldn't you, Papa?

You also wished me to become a painter. And I shall! I'll ask Mama to take me to Paris and then to Italy, where I can learn so much by looking, as you did, at the works of other great artists. I shall use my imagination and my own invention, as you commanded me. I shall work, work and work, as you did. And when I'm good enough, I shall sign my paintings with pride, *Rosario de Goya*.

Listen! The chimes of the clock along the hall. One... two... three... four... five... six! The cruel sun has risen on my first day without you. Someone is sweeping the street outside. Mama will wake and she'll come in presently. Her eyes will be ringed with red, and her body drooping like these wilting flowers. Mariano and sour-faced Gumersinda will come, too, and take charge of the day, and of the funeral. But I don't care what they say. I *shall* sit in the front row of the church at my father's funeral mass.

2
GUMERSINDA
BORDEAUX, 23 APRIL 1828

What a scene met us when we arrived here at the end of last month! El Sordo lying like a decrepit old lion among the tangled bedsheets, pieces of paper covered with drawings scattered all over the floor, the little curly-haired witch perched on the counterpane like a pet bird, and that Weiss woman running around as if she owned the place; ordering the maid hither and thither, making out *she* was going to save my father-in-law's life when it was plain that the old man was finally on his way out, and there was nothing she or her impudent daughter could do to save him, or themselves. The room was filled with El Sordo's liberal friends who had also fled from Spain. Cowards all. Although I must except the Conde de Muguiro; he is a relative of mine and would do nothing dishonourable. I am sure he has perfectly good reasons for being in France.

As soon as we arrived, I made it clear to the Weiss woman precisely *who* was in charge. But I could not prevent my foolish father-in-law from insisting that his precious little pet Rosario was beside him all day long. However, I am fairly certain that after I arrived, at any rate, he was not well enough to act as they wished, although they had long enough to work on him over the years, so one cannot be completely sure.

I must admit that Javier was right in insisting that Mariano and I travelled up here from Madrid although at the time I was set against it. After all, it was most inconvenient, because I was in the middle of fittings for my new wardrobe when the letter came from the old man.

'Your father has been seriously ill so many times,' I said to Javier. 'How can you be sure that *this time* he is dying?'

'I don't know for sure, my dear Gumersinda,' he replied, 'but he is eighty-two years old, and cannot live much longer. He wants us to go to Bordeaux, and he has offered to pay all our expenses, so you must leave at once.'

'What about you?' I inquired as mildly as I could. 'You are his only son. Do you not intend to travel with us?'

'I will follow later. I have affairs to deal with here.'

My husband has many important affairs. *The old fox is as tough as nails. He'll survive this time too*, I thought.

Aloud I said, 'What's the matter with him now? If we must go, can't we wait a week until my fittings are finished? Besides, there is the ball on Friday, remember.'

Javier rarely raises his voice to me, but that day he almost took my head off. 'Fiddle your damned fittings and your ball,' he shouted. 'Listen to his letter.'

And he read out a long complaint from the old man, in which he claimed that he had no sight or strength and ended by begging us to come to France because he was very ill indeed.

'He has bidden us to come to him. You and Mariano will leave at once, and there is an end to it,' Javier said, folding his father's letter and looking more determined than I have ever seen him.

Fancy bidding us to travel from Madrid to Bordeaux, at least nine hundred kilometres, as if it was just up the road! *And* on such dangerous rough roads, *and* in the month of March. I had to persuade Mariano to leave his friends and his card-playing. Like me, he was most reluctant to go, but his father brusquely reminded him that his grandfather had recently given him forty-five thousand francs and that he should show some gratitude. So we had to endure a truly dreadful journey.

But, as I said, in retrospect Javier was right and it was the best thing to do because I feel quite confident that I was able to prevent the old man from giving anything to the Weiss woman and her brat. I needed the eyes of an eagle. She hovered over my father-in-law like a moth and almost succeeded in her plan one afternoon when he suddenly sat up in the bed and declared that he wanted to make another will to ensure that she and Rosario were provided for. But I was alert and managed to convince the old fellow that he had already written a will for her and her bastard. It was a close-run thing, because he was intent on sending for paper and witnesses.

It galls me that the woman is even distantly related to the Goicoecheas. Luckily, few people of my acquaintance knew of the connection when she took up with El Sordo, and I have made sure that a veil remains drawn over it.

The funeral was another ordeal for me. Not only the arrangements and all the fuss with his intellectual friends' speeches, but the constant threat that she and her daughter would disobey our orders and let the world know about their relationship with my father-in-law. Javier had written to make it abundantly clear that neither of them was to appear as important mourners at the funeral. Did they obey him? Not at all. The insolent pair marched right up to the front pew and seated themselves beside us, as if they were family!

I thought Mariano would have a seizure. They wore the blackest black, their faces were as pale as snow, and their eyes red-rimmed. I am quite sure they had applied some cosmetics to make themselves appear tragic. They conspired to show me up. I could not contrive a tear-stained face, though I lowered my head and acted as sorrowfully as I could. The girl did not once look at us but kept dabbing her eyes with her handkerchief and stifling her sobs. What a performance! She should be an actress; that is all she is fit to be. Her mother did not weep or wring her hands. She sat stony-faced throughout the Mass, like a woman whose mind was busy elsewhere. *Her true colours are showing,* I observed. *Now that the old man is gone, she does not have to pretend affection any longer. No doubt she is convinced that her future is secure, and that her acting has achieved her goal. We shall see when the will is read.*

When we got to the cemetery, the pair of them were still to the fore. Worse was to come. When El Sordo was lowered into the tomb, the Weiss woman became crazy and made such loud moanings and cries that all heads turned to look at her. Then her daughter ran forward as if she would throw herself into the tomb. Mariano had to restrain her and lead her away. I shall never forget the embarrassment of it all. Everyone was staring at them, and I could see some people I know shaking their heads and asking questions. I had to do something. I pretended to faint and so everyone's attention turned to me. Mariano rushed back looking most alarmed as he fanned my face to revive me, but I kept my eyes closed and managed to stay as limp as a wet dress.

There is simply no end to that woman's presumption, and her daughter is a defiant little upstart. They will pay for their behaviour; they will pay dearly if I have anything to do with it.

There are times, I have to admit, when I regret my connection with the Goyas. There were problems right from the moment I discovered who my father had chosen to be my husband. Javier was good-looking and personable enough, though not as head-turningly handsome as his besotted father would have it. He is lucky, I suppose, not to have inherited his father's heavy features and figure or his mother's small eyes and thin hair. One of the problems is that the old man spoiled his son, probably because he had managed to survive when all his siblings had died in infancy. You might think I should be sympathetic to such doting, given that Javier and I have been similarly granted only one child, but I am not. I have some sense and I do not hold with pampering. Nor do I permit Javier to dote on Mariano. I most certainly do not want a son who cannot look out for his own interests.

My father and Javier's mother were related and that is how, when I was eighteen years old, he went to see her to arrange a marriage. Papa knew, of course, of Don Francisco Goya's reputation; all Madrid was buzzing with the scandal of his affairs, but Papa knew also that, as Court Painter, El Sordo had amassed a good deal of wealth and that Javier would be the sole beneficiary of his estate. Merchants like my father do not concern themselves overmuch about a man's philandering, as long as he does not desert his wife and family and supports them in good circumstances during his lifetime and afterwards.

It was not as if El Sordo went to the slightest trouble to keep his love affairs secret, or to confine his attention to *majas.* No, he had to have his name linked with one duchess after another, including the Duchess of Alba, and before her the Duchess of Osuna, so they say, and God knows how many others. I have even heard Queen María Luisa's name mentioned! Of course, that woman was no better than a *maja*. One has heard of that mad Roman Emperor, whatever his name was, making a senator of his horse. Or was it a god he made of the dumb animal? What matter? The Queen of Spain elevated a common soldier to the titles of Prince of Peace and Duke of Alcudia and married him off to that poor creature, the Countess of Chinchon. It is intolerable.

My father-in-law's behaviour was even more intolerable because it impacted on me. One wonders if the famous Court Painter demanded their favours in part-payment for deigning to paint noble ladies' portraits. One also wonders what such elegant and well-bred ladies saw in a low-bred, deaf man with the coarse face of an uncouth peasant.

When I married Javier in 1805, Madrid was still bubbling with rumours about the mysterious death of Maria Teresa Cayetana, Duchess of Alba, even though the event had occurred over three years before. There were those who said that the Queen, in fit of jealousy, had had the Duchess poisoned in revenge for the latter's affair with Don Manuel Godoy, while others, mainly at Court, maintained that her servants had killed her in order to benefit all the sooner from her crazy will. Imagine leaving that incredible wealth to such lowly people as her chambermaid and some miserable black child she had adopted! Of course, every time these rumours were given an airing, my father-in-law's disgraceful relationship with the Duchess got a good outing as well. If the gossips had known that she had willed Javier ten reales a day for the rest of his life, I am sure they would have a great deal more speculation with which to amuse themselves at our expense. I really have had such a lot to put up with since I married the son of Don Francisco Goya.

'Papa wishes to paint our portraits,' Javier announced on the evening of our betrothal. 'He has decided to paint my mother too. He will have a family portrait gallery then because he already has many portraits of himself.'

Javier laughed, delighted with his clever father. I should have been pleased, I suppose, but I was not charmed that the famous artist would paint me.

'Why does your father not make a joint portrait of yourself and your mother?'

'No, he specifically said that he wishes to paint each of us separately – as a wedding gift. This is to be, you understand, only one of the wedding gifts he intends to give us, so do not worry.'

Thus I had to resign myself to going to El Sordo's studio, to enter the very place where seductions probably took place. It was a large room on the first floor, filled with enormous canvases, jugs of brushes and tubs of colours. There was a printing press in one corner and also a stack of copper plates. A red velvet couch and some damask-covered chairs provided seating.

My father-in-law was standing by an easel at a tall north window. He was wearing a long, green velvet coat tied in the middle with a gold tasselled belt, white silk stockings and fine breeches. I was surprised by such elegant attire, but I supposed he had to dress like that when he was at the Royal Palace.

'The Court Painter is weary of painting the nobility and has decided to paint his own family for a change,' he said.

There was an ink and chalk drawing of Doña Josefa on the easel. I had a good look at it while El Sordo was fussing with his brushes and colours. He had pictured her sitting sideways on an upright chair, wearing a most unbecoming shawl and bonnet. She was shown with a slight double chin and the ruddy round cheeks of a peasant. I certainly did not want such a mean portrayal of myself.

I had to endure sitting, without moving a muscle, for hours on end, while he sketched and then painted me. Since I had not wanted the portrait in the first place, I had not been inclined to give much consideration to which of my dresses and bonnets to wear, but Javier had persuaded me that a portrait is for posterity and that I should put on my best clothes and look my most pleasing.

'Please do not wear one of your sulky looks,' he begged me.

I am sure I do not know what he meant. I did my best, as I have always done, to please my husband. I wore my crimson silk dress, imported from France, and took care to choose my most flattering bonnet. As I sat there in the studio, I attempted to cast my mind on more agreeable subjects than El Sordo while he stared at me, and made his disgusting grunting noises. (I call him El Sordo privately. I would never, of course, call him that in front of Javier.) I was not in the least inclined to make conversation with a deaf man; with an adulterer.

What miserable little copper roundels he made of us! What about the one he did of me, his only son's wife? He paid a great deal more attention to the pink ribbon on my bonnet than to my features. And he did not even show my beautiful new dress beyond the very top of it. Really, I need not have bothered taking it from my closet: worst of all, he portrayed me as discontented and ill-tempered.

When Javier brought the object into our house some weeks later and showed it to me, I screamed. But he would hear nothing against his father.

'You must have worn one of your scowls,' was all he would say.

Really, one would have expected one's new husband to support one against such treatment. Javier has had to learn to understand that I demand respect.

Javier's likeness is equally skimpily dealt with, but at least he was given an agreeable face. As for the other portrait of Doña Josefa, which El Sordo made that same year! He has her looking like some ancient chambermaid, with her hair tucked away under a cap. I know for certain that my mother-in-law wore her blue figured-silk gown for that portrait. When I consider the large size and the sumptuous detail of the portraits of his aristocratic patrons, and compare them to our tiny things, I really have to question El Sordo's respect for his own family.

Doña Josefa was so much superior in every way to her husband. That is no wonder because she, like us, was from the Aragonese nobility; although admittedly the Bayeaus were somewhat impoverished in later generations. Doña Josefa had breeding and good manners and, by the saints, I cannot understand why she married El Sordo, never mind how she endured his baseless arrogance, his uncivilised bullfighting mania, and his innumerable affairs. He was certainly no great catch. It is impossible to understand why her brother even considered giving his sister in marriage to such a bumpkin. Why, he could not even provide a house for his bride; Don Francisco Bayeu, it is well known, had to support the couple for years. And El Sordo depended on Doña Josefa's brother for everything else also – introductions, commissions, everything. Without Don Francisco Bayeu, Señor Goya could not have survived. Without his brother-in-law, El Sordo would, no doubt, have spent his life gilding frames like his father in

Saragossa, or swaggering and fighting in the back streets and bordellos of Madrid.

Doña Josefa had more breeding and good manners in her little finger than El Sordo had in his whole body. Not that I would ever say anything of the kind to Javier. He, poor fool, still thinks that his father was the greatest genius in Spain and the best father in the universe. He refuses to hear a single word against him. Even when Doña Josefa lay dying and, in her delirium, finally gave vent to her righteous anger against her husband, Javier would insist that she did not know what she was saying. I have had a long, hard struggle to try to disabuse my husband of his false faith in his father, made longer and harder by the old man's flamboyant acts of largesse.

Our house at Calle de Les Reyes, for example. It was one of his wedding presents to us. And the eighty-four thousand reales he deposited in the Royal Life Pension Fund for us was another wedding gift. It stuck in my throat, having to be grateful for that house. Because he had given it to us, he felt he could visit us unannounced any time he felt like, to be with his beloved son, and no doubt to check on how his darling was being treated. And, my goodness, when Mariano was born, you would think it was a miracle. *A grandson. Another Goya*, he kept saying like a silly parrot. He came round to the house every day for about six months and sat by the crib watching the child's every breath. And he interfered with the nurse's work, telling her to give the child all sorts of strange foods *to build up his strength*. I had to put a stop to that.

When I gently complained to Javier about his father's obsession with the child, he said: 'You must be understanding and remember that Papa lost many children before I was born. It will be all right when Mariano reaches the age of five; Papa will feel confident that he will survive. Until then you must be patient, my dear.'

Five years of El Sordo's endless solicitation about my son was just too much, and there were many times when I instructed the servants to inform him that we were not at home. The interfering old devil then questioned Javier as to why I took Mariano out so often and commented that he thought that too much running around was not good for the child's health.

'What is this my father says about your not being at home when he calls to see Mariano? Manuela tells me that you are in your room and that you give orders to her to tell my father lies and so deny him the opportunity to see his own grandson. You are a deceitful woman, Gumersinda. I never want to hear of such lies again. We owe everything to my father. Pray do not forget that.'

Javier never spoke to me again in such a fashion. I was much cleverer in my dealings with El Sordo after that. For example, when he wanted to sign over almost everything he possessed to the child, I managed to persuade Javier to stop him. I argued that if all that fortune were put in trust for Mariano, we could not have access to any of it. Not a reale! In the midst of famine and war, we should have starved. Well, perhaps not exactly starved, but we might have had to go without some things.

My young cousins sometimes ask me what it was like when that little Corsican upstart and his army overran our great country and turned Madrid into a slaughterhouse. I keep my mouth shut. I will tell nobody that my own father-in-law spent half his time hiding in his studio and the other half painting portraits of the tyrant and of his retinue. Oh, of course, he put it about afterwards that he had gone to Saragossa to support his own people, but the portraits are there to prove that he was a miserable collaborator. He may fool some people with his grand gestures – those paintings of the second of May and the third of May, planning to hang them from triumphal arches when our own monarch was restored – but he did not fool me for one instant. The man was an opportunist from first to last. From his insinuation into the Bayeu family, to his notorious affairs with duchesses and the like, to his craven collaboration with the French. There are no other words for him. Opportunist, adulterer, collaborator! I know that one should not speak ill of the dead, but I do not care.

My poor mother-in-law was subjected to the most dreadful life. What with all those pregnancies and infant funerals, endless scandals and rumours of her husband's affairs, his lengthy and unexplained absences from Madrid and, on top of all that, the mysterious illness that left him as deaf as a doorpost and unable to work for months on end. One could speculate about the nature and the cause of that illness, and indeed some people have done so on occasion, and in my hearing. Really, being subjected to those rumours was too much to bear. I am certain that my mother-in-law heard them too. It is a wonder that Doña Josefa did not take leave of her senses.

I shall never forget those days and weeks when she lay dying in that oppressive room in Calle del Desengáno. She would have us by her day and night, and Javier wore himself out sitting for hours on end by her bedside. He would come home fatigued and tell me some of the things his mother had been rambling on about. I could not be there myself obviously, day in and day out, because I had so much to attend to. I hoped that when Javier heard the things his mother had said, he would finally realise what a scoundrel his father was, but, as I have already said, he dismissed his mother's words as delirium, and simply would not believe a single thing against his father. I am not for a moment suggesting that my husband did not love his mother. No son could have shown more devotion, but Javier is as blind as his father was deaf, and nobody could make him see the truth about that dreadful man. I did try, in my own quiet way of course.

'Where do you think your father is?' I would ask him. 'Why is he not at his wife's bedside when she is dying and constantly asking for him? What could be more important at such a time?'

But Javier would just shake his head and say that his father was one of the hardest workers in all Spain, and that he had the most important obligations at Court, which he could neither avoid nor postpone.

'Please be so good as to remember, Gumersinda, that Papa is the Court Painter,' he would say. 'He has many commitments. He comes home as often as he can and spends what free time he has at Mama's bedside. What else can he do? Mama has been ill for months. The doctors do not know what is wrong with her. He cannot simply stop painting.'

I was so infuriated by Javier's blindness that one day I reminded him that when he was a child and suffering from some kind of pox, his father had given up work entirely and had even bothered the King himself with details of the illness. But all Javier said to that was that his father was not Court Painter at that time and that he had not had the same obligations. After that, I gave up trying to take the blindfold from my husband's eyes. I devoted my energies to discovering where my father-in-law was spending his time when he was not at Court or in the palaces of the nobles he painted. I had a good idea what he was up to and I was proved right before Doña Josefa was long in her grave.

My father knew Señor Isidore Weiss. They had had business dealings for a number of years.

'He is of German extraction, but he is a good Catholic, nonetheless, and a successful merchant,' Papa told me.

Papa is a good judge of character. Had he known his intentions, my father could have warned Señor Weiss against marrying Leocadia Zorilla y Golarza, who, I am ashamed to admit, is distantly related to my mother.

'Señor Weiss has taken on a strong-headed young wife, poor man,' I heard Papa telling Mama one day. 'She has the look of an unbroken filly; and is not shy about announcing her opinions. She will bring trouble to Señor Weiss if he does not quickly rein her in, mark my words.'

How right Papa was! Within a year we heard that the couple had produced a child, and another one a year later, and hard on the heels of that news, came the first rumblings of Señor Weiss's disquiet about his young wife's extramarital behaviour! I think it was around 1807 or 1808 that the marriage took place and the elder child, a son, I believe, was hardly three years old when Leocadia upped and left the poor misguided man and settled herself into Calle del Desengáno. One does not have to be a genius to work out what the Court Painter had been up to while his wife lay dying at home. It sounds a dreadful thing to admit, but I am glad that my dear Mama was not alive to see the scandal her relative created. I simply refused to take Mariano to that house after that scheming woman moved in there.

'You can go to visit your father if you must,' I told Javier, 'but I cannot come with you while that whore is in residence.'

My husband would beg me to let our son see his grandfather. I relented and permitted Javier to take Mariano to visit El Sordo from time to time, but I insisted that the Weiss woman was not present at their meetings. I had no intention of allowing my child to be contaminated.

The only thing that could possibly be said in El Sordo's favour is that, for once, he had the grace not to flaunt the affair. In fact, so well did he cover his traces and keep up the pretence that she was his housekeeper that not a soul guessed what was going on. And to this day, Javier just refuses to believe that the hussy was anything other than his father's housekeeper. Where does he think the child came from, for God's sake? I mean, how can he possibly go along with the myth that Rosario is the offspring of the poor cuckold Señor Weiss? The child even has El Sordo's stubborn chin and unruly hair. I tell you there is no accounting for the stupidity or the blindness of men. They are like blinkered mules.

After Doña Josefa's death, El Sordo divided all the property and signed over half of it to Javier. We had already inherited all my mother-in-law's estate and so we were quite well-off. And not before time. I had had enough of having to accept handouts from the Court Painter. It was high time that Javier got his hands on a decent amount of money so that I could invest it, for our future and for our son's future. I am not a merchant's daughter for nothing. All those years I was so frustrated at not having sufficient funds to invest to make our fortune. My father is the most long-lived of men and I am still awaiting the remainder of our inheritance from him.

El Sordo made a fortune, it has to be admitted, but he spent a lot of money foolishly – on his carriages, his French jackets, his English boots, and on other expenses I prefer not to guess at. There was one time, however, when he ran out of money and wanted to borrow from Javier.

'Let him go to his rich patrons,' I said. 'We need all we have for our son's future. In any case, what needs has an old man, with his own house and a fine fat salary from the King?'

Javier begged me to reconsider, but I managed to convince him that we would suffer a serious loss of interest if we released the money from the bond. And that was that.

I planned a way to get rid of them both from Madrid. It took some time, but it worked.

'Do you not think that the country air would be good for your father?' I suggested to Javier. 'After all, he is not working so much now and he needs to rest a little. He should buy a place outside Madrid and live quietly, as befits a man of his age.'

'My dear wife, how thoughtful you are. I'll tell Papa about your idea. I'm sure you're right and that fresh air would do him a lot of good,' Javier said, beaming at me.

'Please do not say it was my suggestion. You know how independent-minded he is. He *must* think it's his own idea.'

Thus, when I heard that El Sordo had decided to move out of Madrid with his *housekeeper* and buy a house in the countryside, I was very pleased indeed and much relieved. Now the disgraceful liaison would not be conducted right in front of our faces, as it were. I vowed I would not set foot in that house. And I kept my promise to myself while El Sordo was alive. Not even when he deeded La Quinta to my dear Mariano did I relent. I may visit the place now – I believe it has been much extended and improved – but before I go there, I will have to insist on the removal of the abominable paintings, which I have heard cover the walls. To think that when he was an innocent child, Mariano had to see such depravities.

It also disturbs me to know that when Mariano went to visit El Sordo he witnessed his grandfather treating the little schemer as his own daughter.

'Mariano worships that little enchantress Rosario,' Javier announced one time when they came back from a visit to La Quinta; 'he cannot be kept away from her. Today he spent hours playing with her in the garden.'

What did I say about men and blindness? Before I could open my mouth, Javier hushed me.

'Now Gumersinda, my dear,' he protested, 'please don't let your imagination run away with you. Papa is an old man; his housekeeper is a young married woman, who, although she does not live with her husband at present, has three children by him, one of whom, Rosario, happens to be living with her in Papa's house.'

I closed my mouth, for I could see there was nothing to be gained by speaking the truth. I became all the more determined to ensure that the little bastard in no way compromised my son's rightful inheritance, and that her mother would not get a single reale which should belong to Mariano. And to us, of course.

Mariano inherited La Quinta when he was just seventeen, much earlier than I expected. I knew that the wily fox had written the deed simply in order to avoid the confiscation of his property. Really, I do not know how he escaped! Besides the little matter of his collaboration with the French, there were those disgraceful paintings of naked women it is said that he made for that scoundrel Godoy. I was amazed when he escaped the Inquisitors. I have it on good authority that the Weiss woman was in almost as much danger of persecution as El Sordo for her radical opinions. Had the Inquisitors known about those also the pair of them would surely have been imprisoned. What business has a woman got having radical opinions? Our job is to marry well and thereafter to ensure that our husbands and our children are as healthy and as prosperous as possible. We can have as many opinions as we like on those matters, but it is most certainly not our place to concern ourselves with affairs of the state, or to have any opinions about politics, radical or otherwise. God gave men and women different brains for different purposes, and if they insist on crossing into the other's realm of action and influence, there can be nothing but trouble.

If I had been one of the Inquisitors, I would have ensured that she was locked up with him, and all his sordid paintings and prints destroyed, burnt on a bonfire. And I would have gone out there and thrown that miserable roundel he painted of me right on the top of the flames.

I cannot understand why a respected member of the clergy, a consecrated priest, should have given asylum to El Sordo when he was forced into hiding. Don José de Duas y Latre will have a lot to answer for when he meets his Divine Master. A priest like that should have been excommunicated. He was just as bad as the scandal-giver, and he allowed El Sordo to escape retribution.

Javier did seem shocked when we discovered that the Weiss woman had turned up in Bordeaux and had moved herself and her children into his father's house. I expect he was so taken aback because he could no longer fool himself that she was merely a housekeeper. Apparently, she has made no pretence of such a position in Bordeaux. And, insult of insults, she tried to convince El Sordo to adopt Rosario. When Javier informed me of this latest scandal, I was furious. I had quite a lot of inquiries to make regarding the inheritance rights of adopted children.

I surprised Javier by insisting that Mariano should take every opportunity to visit his grandfather in France. He was twenty-one by then and could quite easily travel that distance alone. He came back from his visits to Bordeaux full of talk about the Rosario creature, how she and his grandfather were inseparable, how El Sordo spent hours making pictures for her, how she was the only one allowed into his studio while he was working. And then, near the end, how El Sordo was painting a large picture of her, which he called *The Milkmaid of Bordeaux.* You can imagine how disturbing such stories were to me!

'Have you told your grandpapa that you mean to be married into the aristocracy?' I asked Mariano. 'And have you mentioned that such a marriage will need a great deal of money?'

But my foolish son just laughed and said that he had plenty of time to think of marriage! Had he not been a great strong fellow, standing a head taller than me, I would have shaken him.

'What does Señora Weiss's daughter look like now?' I asked as casually as I could.

'She's rather a pretty girl, I suppose.'

'And how does she behave?'

'Well, although she appears quite delicate, she has a determined character. Just like Grandpapa! She gets her way in that house without having to raise her voice. I have never seen Grandpapa so obedient to any person. She seems to work some magic on him.'

You can imagine the state of my heartbeat when I heard that! I had the wildest notion of going straight to Bordeaux and poisoning the wretched little witch. However, I reminded myself that we had already inherited almost everything El Sordo possessed and that he could not have much more wealth secreted away. But with him one never knew. He could have had a hoard. Had he not spent his entire life accumulating wealth? And, besides, word had come to me that he had consulted a certain Don Joaquin Ferrer, a banker, regarding the sale of his lithographs in France. No doubt he made a good deal of money from that deal, and that money rightly belongs to my son. As do the considerable sums to be made when all the paintings are sold.

Two years ago El Sordo suddenly reappeared like a bad omen in Madrid. He had come to request permission from the King to retire, if you don't mind! He had his salary converted into a pension of about fifty thousand reales, Javier told me. With that sum he could live comfortably in Bordeaux and take care of the Weiss witch and her children. What a pity! Had he been impoverished, I doubt if she would have stayed with him. As it was, I am sure she held on until his death in the hope that he would provide well for her and for their daughter.

Javier was inconsolable when his father died. The man was eighty-two years old, for the love of God! How much longer did he expect the old monster to live? Better men than El Sordo have died at a much younger age. Men who had lived good clean lives; men who had not driven their wives into the grave. I do my best to appear suitably sorrowful, but when I am alone in my boudoir, I cannot stop smiling in my mirror, and my heart is as light as a bird's.

'I didn't realise you cared so much for Papa, my dear,' Javier said last night. 'I had always thought you did not wholly approve of him.'

I just smiled weakly at him and looked grief-stricken. My husband is very pleased with me, and I am more than pleased with myself. The Weiss woman and her bastard will get nothing. I would not be surprised if she thinks she might persuade Mariano to let them live at La Quinta again. Some hope! Serves her right. She should have stayed with her own husband. And she should not have borne a bastard Goya. Javier will pay them off with a few hundred reales. I shall see to it.

3

LEOCADIA
BORDEAUX, 24 APRIL 1828

How good it is to see you, my dear Isabel. Thank you so much for breaking your journey back from Paris to see me. I sorely need you now to console and counsel me. It is over a week since my dear Francisco was taken from me, since his poisonous daughter-in-law and grandson deigned to come to Bordeaux to see him before he died. Not that they rushed to be at his side. He had to write and beg them to come. His son, Javier, did not bother to come with them so my poor Francisco died without seeing his only son on whom he doted. Oh what a relief it is to be able to speak frankly to someone who cares for me. It's been a nightmare since Francisco died. I cannot tell you the indignities we have had to suffer, Rosario and me, at the hands of those people.

Of course, I'll miss Francisco for the rest of my days, and so will our daughter, but … do you know what's eating my brain? I do not know what is to become of us now that he is gone from us. The day he became paralysed, about two weeks before he died (although we did not actually realise for some time that he was paralysed) he lay for hours looking at his hand, as if he was stupefied. He seemed very agitated. Presently he grunted: 'Fetch Rosario and bring two witnesses. I must make another will. Quickly, Leocadia, Quickly,'

Since he had so often mentioned his intention to leave us well-off, I had assumed he had already made a will in our favour. *Another one?* I said to myself. *How much more will he leave us in this new will?* I sent the maid immediately to fetch Rosario and two witnesses, but as bad luck would have it, the vixen Gumersinda, his daughter-in-law, who was writing at a table in the far corner of the room (probably making an inventory of the furniture) overheard Francisco and the witch rushed forward and took his hand, arch actress that she is, and cooed and smoothed his brow, and assured him that he had already made such a will. She practically knocked me down to get to him. She pulled his face towards her, so he could read her lips only and so that he could not see a word of my protests. I could have wrung her scrawny little neck.

Francisco looked confused and tried to speak, but she kept on reassuring him until he nodded in exhaustion and closed his eyes.

'Don Francisco, everything is in order so you must not upset yourself. You are so tired and need to rest now,' she cooed as if she cared one whit if the poor man was dead or alive.

I determined that as soon as she had left the room, I would fetch paper and Rosario and two witnesses. But by the time she had gone, Francisco had fallen into unconsciousness. Although he did regain consciousness from time to time after that, he was incapable of writing his name.

I heartily regret now that I did not wrench the interfering baggage away from him. What harm if he had already made a will for us? Better to be sure than sorry – that has always been my motto. Had I acted, I would not be so worried now, *and* I would have had the deep satisfaction of seeing that vixen with her snobbish nose put out of joint.

Francisco lingered on in that paralysed condition for two weeks, as I have told you. That wily Gumersinda and her brat Mariano were here all that time and, by God, they did their best to keep Rosario and me from speaking with him, or spending any time alone with him. No doubt, they were afraid he would recover sufficiently to make another will in our favour. You understand my fears, don't you my dear friend? Not that you need to worry about money or a roof over your head. Your father has left you very well-off and you have no siblings or other relatives to squabble over the inheritance.

Rosario? Well, you know that she was the apple of her father's eye. She is desolate, now that she has no father, no protector, but she is also a pragmatist, like her father. She's as stubborn as he was, although I suppose I can't blame her for being like him. Do you know what she did the night he died? Spent all night alone with his corpse! She was sitting by his bed when I came into the room at dawn, her small form bent intently towards him, as if they had been having a nightlong conversation. Her face, when she turned to look at me in the lamplight, was pale, but no tears streaked it.

'We shall sit at the front of the church, right beside Gumersinda and Mariano, Mama,' she announced. 'I will not have it otherwise. I'm Papa's child, no matter what Mariano or anyone else says, and I *shall* be placed among the chief mourners. Just as you must be.'

I hadn't noticed until then that she has his determined lower lip, his unflinching eyes, as if he had somehow transferred them to her during the night. You saw her this afternoon when you arrived, Isabel. Don't you agree that she looks so much like her father? There are those, of course, who would deny that she's anything like him. That would suit their purposes.

The day before he died, she was a girl, young for her fourteen years, lively, curious, playful. The following morning she had become the serious, determined young woman you see today. Whatever happened during that night she sat by her father's corpse has changed her. She seems to have taken on some of his iron, but still I fear life will not be easy for her.

We did take our places at the front of the church. Rosario took my arm and we marched right up to the front pew to sit with the others. I could feel Gumersinda's eyes scorching me. It kills her that we're relatives. It makes it harder for her to pretend that I'm a servant in this house. Will their jealousy and resentment of me never end? I've had such a lot of suffering and abuse to bear, my dear friend, because of my relationship with Francisco de Goya.

I was proud of my daughter that day: the way she held up her head defiantly and ignored Gumersinda's and Mariano's displeasure. She's a true child of her father; of that there is no doubt. I thought she was going to strike one of the priests who ignored both of us when he came down from the altar to offer condolences to the family. I had to put my hand on her arm to still her. What do I care for the approval or recognition of priests, or of anyone else? Yet when ignorant people treat me like his housekeeper, I have to admit, Isabel, that even after all these years, it still riles me. But then I say to myself: *Why should I upset myself? I was mistress of the house at La Quinta, as I was here in Bordeaux until Gumersinda arrived. Francisco chose me as his wifely companion for the last sixteen years of his life. There was many a disappointed aristocratic lady and* maja *jealous of me, that is for certain.*

Please do not suppose that I think badly of Francisco. But there are some things I wish he had done. God forgive me for thinking like this at such a time, but really he *should* have assisted me to get rid of Isidoro, and to have my marriage annulled. Had he done so, he could have married me. After all, did I not sacrifice my youth and beauty to live with him – a deaf and often cantankerous old man? That was not easy, Isabel, as you can imagine. I don't think Francisco ever really appreciated the sacrifices I made for his sake. You're lucky that you never married. You've no idea of the amount of trouble men bring into one's life. How wise you were to avoid all that.

Excuse me, dear friend, for talking about intimate matters, but I've had nobody to listen to me for such a long time and I feel as if I will burst if I can't unburden myself now. It's some time since we last saw each other. I cannot remember how long … Before I moved to La Quinta? … Really? *That* long ago? Goodness, how time flies! I *did* write to you from time to time, though, didn't I? You didn't get *any* letters from me? That's strange. Oh well, you have no idea how busy I was at that time. It wasn't easy looking after such an eccentric and wilful man as Francisco, or dealing with an extremely energetic child like Rosario. And I had my older son, Guillermo, with me some of the time too. He missed me and would not stay with his father. Perhaps it's difficult for you to understand such things, Isabel, not having had any great events in your own life.

After the first months of passion were over, and especially after Rosario was born, Francisco retreated from me somewhat, and I had quite a job to get him to take enough notice of me.

Although he still desired me physically, he was often impatient with me, saying that he could not deal with what he called my *moods*. He should talk about moods! He also claimed that I was too wilful and argumentative. I suppose his wife, Doña Josefa, was as quiet as a lamb and did what she was told. Well, she was from another generation. I assure you, Isabel, it took the patience of a saint to live with that man. But it was also a privilege, to be in the company of a genius. To feel his enormous energy fill the house, to listen to his knowledgeable discussions with his friends, to see how little he was awed by aristocracy, to witness his searing depiction of stupidity and vanity in society. I have never met a man like him. And despite our quarrels I loved him dearly. I hope he loved me too.

He spent what free time he had with Don Cean Bermudez and his other intellectual and business friends, discussing politics and intrigues and the making of money. He seemed to be able to follow their conversation easily, he was a genius at lip reading. Oh yes, painting was not the only thing which interested him, he loved intrigue, literature, new ideas. He was also very interested in finding means of increasing his wealth. His close associate Don Gaspar Melchor Jovellanes advised him to place funds in the new bank of San Carlos. I trust that this advice served Francisco well and that Rosario and I will benefit, at least to some extent. I am not greedy, I simply need enough to meet our needs from now on.

The rest of the time, when he was not painting, he spent play-acting with Rosario. He spoiled that girl. His whole face would change when he would see her coming. He didn't look at *me* with such tenderness. She had him wound around her little finger. No wonder Mariano was jealous. That brat will do well from his grandfather's will. He has already got thousands of reales from Francisco, as well as a lot of property and paintings. Will there be enough left over for my needs? That's my fear. However, Francisco promised me faithfully that he would look after Rosario and me. I had to bring up the subject quite often. Nonetheless, I have taken the precaution of asking an acquaintance of mine to go to Madrid to discover what provision Francisco has made for us. Pedro will report to me very soon.

When I woke on the morning after his death, I cursed the birds for singing, the sun for rising so heartlessly, and the damnable cocks for crowing as if my world had not been turned inside out. The servants made their same early morning noises, the wind whispered through the vines on the terrace, as is does almost every day. There was no pity for me anywhere. My great bulwark was gone. My daughter is fatherless. I am alone in the world.

What a magnificent funeral he had at Grande Chartreuse. No more than he deserved, of course. You should have seen it, Isabel, like an exiled prince he was, surrounded by the most distinguished exiles from our country, including Juan Bautista and the Conde de Muguiro. Ten priests and a bishop concelebrated his Requiem Mass and the church was overflowing with notables. *The greatest Spanish painter of this century,* they called him in the many eulogies. *A fearless, uncompromising genius who was true to his own vision. A giant among artists. Friend and confidant of the most enlightened aristocrats, sought after by the finest intellectuals in Spain, as well as in France.* Not so communicative in his own house, I'm afraid.

After the Mass, he was buried in the Muguiro family vault. He had taken care to arrange that through Javier's in-laws.

'I may have come from an obscure background,' he often declared, 'but I shall be buried with nobility, where I rightly belong.'

And just beside him, in the next tomb, is Don Martin Goicoechea – Javier's father-in-law. Whatever I may think of Gumersinda, I have to admit that the Goicoecheas are a distinguished family.

Isabel, it was impossible to restrain myself when they lowered my Francisco into that vault. I felt that my past and, more importantly, my future were being buried with him. People stared at me; some of them tut-tutted. Gumersinda's and Mariano's faces were as red and wobbling as a turkey cock's. But why should I pretend? Everybody here *knows* that I was his wife – in all but name. There were fishwives in Madrid who made much of the scandal when Isidoro accused me of illicit behaviour. They insinuated that I had seduced Francisco while Doña Josefa lay dying; tattled that I could hardly wait for her casket to be removed from the family home before I moved in. It is truly dreadful to have been the butt of such vicious tongues for so much of my life. Doña Josefa was dead for ages before I went to live in that house. In any case, what I do is my own business and nobody else's.

Before I went to his house to work as his housekeeper, I knew of his wild reputation, as, no doubt, you did yourself, Isabel. In those days, I was on quite good terms with Gumersinda, and she told me often how difficult she found her father-in-law. *His manners are provincial and clumsy*, she said, *and he is as petulant as a child*. That termagant! Accusing anyone of petulance!

Everyone in Madrid had heard the rumours of Francisco's younger days, about his unruliness, his quarrelsomeness, the

brawls he got into. There was even some story that he had
knifed another man to death, a fellow artist, in Saragossa, or
Cadiz. The location changed each time I heard the story, as
did the manner of the alleged killing. One time it was with a
knife, another time the fellow had apparently been killed with
a musket, and yet a third story said that death had resulted
from a blow from a candlestick. People are so often jealous of
men so much their superior. They try to denigrate them in any
way they can. I cannot abide scandal mongers.

Then there was the rumour about Francisco, when he was
a young man of about twenty, abducting a nun and running
off to Rome with her. There he was supposed to have climbed
the dome of St. Peter's. He may well have tried to climb the
dome, but a nun! I don't believe a word of it. No doubt you
heard the endless gossip about the number of women with
whom he was supposed to have had affairs – duchesses as well
as *majas*. Why, it was even whispered that he used to seduce
his female models in his studio, covering the statue of the
Virgin with a cloth while he made love to them! Excuse my
mentioning such things to you, Isabel. *Worse than the Duke
of Wellington for womanising,* they said. Don't you remember
that even Queen María Luisa's name was linked to his? I don't
believe that for an instant, do you? That woman was too
besotted with Don Manuel Godoy to have eyes, or time, for
anyone else. Besides, Francisco was neither young enough nor
good-looking enough for her.

The Duchess of Alba – she must be dead for at least a
quarter of a century – well, she was supposed to be another
of his conquests. I have my doubts about that rumour too.
It's well enough known that her preference was for handsome
young *toreros*, musicians, actors and the like. What would she
have seen in an old deaf man?

I never questioned Francisco about his former life. Why should I? A man must have his privacy. As indeed must a woman. And a genius must have whatever he needs. That's the way I look at it. A man like Francisco de Goya cannot be judged like other men. He is *not* like other men. He's as different from them as a taper is from a star.

Francisco treated me well. I never wanted for anything for myself or for Rosario. He made no fuss about Guillermo living with us here in Bordeaux these past few years and paid no attention to what the scandalmongers spread around about me. And he agreed to my wish to move out of Madrid. Of course, Gumersinda thinks that the move was *her* idea.

We had some good years at La Quinta del Sordo. It's a great pity that you never came to visit us there, Isabel. Really? You should have known you didn't need a special invitation. I would have been only too pleased to have received you. At any time that was convenient.

It was the most beautiful house and garden. I should say the house *was* beautiful until Francisco got to work on the walls of most of the rooms. Isabel, he *flung* paint at those walls. He scooped colours from tubs at his feet and daubed them onto the walls with sponges or rags and sometimes even with a long-handled mop! Do you know what he used to make strokes with? His thumbs! Honestly, he was like one possessed. He worked non-stop all day long, covering an entire wall of maybe thirty metres in one day, and then often worked into the night. There was not much time or energy left over for an intimate life with me, I can tell you. It's a wonder I did not take a *cortejo*.

Such horrible scenes as he created on those walls! Witches, hobbledehoys, devil-worshippers – enough to give you nightmares. But I just had to keep my mouth closed and let him do as he pleased. It wasn't easy for me, as you know. I learned what I had to do in order to have a peaceful life, and that was to keep out of his way; make no protest about the monstrosities he painted, or about the money he lavished on the garden, or indeed about anything else he wanted to do. As long as I said nothing, everything went smoothly. Why, he almost purred like a big cuddly cat! It had not always been so.

When I first went to live in his house in Calle Valverde, I was dreadfully unhappy. You know what it was like for me then, for we met often to discuss my problems. It was impossible to ignore the foul remarks I would hear about myself every time I walked on the Prado with you or with one of my cousins. Not only did I have to endure the gossips, but I had so few occasions to wear my fine dresses, because Francisco would not allow me to accompany him anywhere. For the most part, all my fine mantillas and combs and fans lay on my table and nobody of consequence could see me wearing them. Do you know that he did not permit me to meet those who came to our house to sit for their portraits? It was almost as if he was ashamed of me. I tackled him about it once and his reply was that Doña Josefa had never once interfered in his working life, and that *she* was the model of an ideal wife.

I tell you, Isabel, he ran a campaign of terror in his studio. His poor models were not allowed to move a muscle, and if they twitched as much as an eyelid, he would fly into such a rage and fling his palette to the ground. I could hear him raging from outside the door. Nobody could interrupt him. If I so much as put my head around the door to see who he had with him, he would fly into a fury.

Still, I must admit Francisco worked very quickly, often completing a portrait in a day. He commanded a large fee, too. I seem to recall that he charged one thousand reales for a sketch and about twelve thousand for the completed portrait, which in those years was as much as an annual salary. Although he did only three or four portraits a year, we had more than enough to live on. As you know, he did a lot more besides portrait painting, so he made a great deal of money. Francisco was so clever about conserving his wealth; not that he was in the least bit mean, you understand. He supported his old mother for years as well as his sisters. He was a family man in that regard.

You might well wonder why I tied myself down with an old man. To tell the truth, I did not have a great deal of choice at the time. I was very pretty, if I say so myself, when I was younger. Indeed my looks have been compared more than once to the Duchess of Alba's. I never saw her but I have heard that she was extremely beautiful.

'I am an old man; my wife is dead; I am deaf, and some say that I am difficult,' – that is how he put it when he interviewed me for the job as his housekeeper. 'You are a beautiful young woman. Why do you think you would be content to run the house of an old widower?'

'I need to support myself and my children,' I replied, wondering how deaf people understood one. He motioned me to speak more slowly and I repeated my answer.

He followed my lips with his eyes.

'Why is that, may I ask? That you need to support yourself, I mean. Where is your husband, the father of your children?'

I could not tell him that I had walked out on my husband. Four years married to that man was more than enough, I can tell you, so I stared at the floor and said nothing.

'I see,' he said with a smile, and he looked at me with such intensity that I blushed and turned away.

So you see, Isabel, it is not true that Francisco enticed me away from Isidoro, or that we were already lovers while Doña Josefa was dying, or that the affair hastened her death. My marriage was over by the time I came to work for Francisco, and his wife had been dead for months. I started out as his housekeeper and did not become his lover for quite some time. He did not try to seduce me or to trick me in any way.

This is how our affair began. I was cooking *Puchero en olla* one day when he came striding into the kitchen.

'Señora,' he said, 'I need a model for a painting I am about to start. I wish you to pose for me. Of course, you will be relieved of your housekeeping duties during the time you spend modelling. I shall employ another woman in your place.'

I agreed to pose for him without a second's consideration. Without even inquiring what kind of posing he had in mind. Now you may be wondering, Isabel, why a woman of my background was willing to do such a thing. Was I not compromising myself? To tell you the truth, I surprised myself by how quickly and how willingly I agreed. I think it might have been because I had just left my husband a few months before, and so I felt very daring. I was ready to embark on any adventure which offered itself. And what an adventure my life became! For by the time the painting was finished, the painter was in love with me.

Rosario was born eighteen months later. Until my pregnancy was obvious, I managed to hide our affair, but when it became known, I had a terrible time of it. I was unable to go out, for fear of meeting one of Isidoro's spies, and because I could not bear the whispers and sniggers that followed me in the street. That is why, during those months, I could not see you, my dear Isabel, or any of my old friends. I was like a prisoner in that house and I became extremely depressed.

One sweltering evening, Teresa — she was our servant atthat time, a foul-mouthed and insolent girl from Saragossa whom Francisco favoured — I got rid of her later on — announced that the Monsignor from Saint Benedict's desired to see me in the salon. I wrapped my shawl around me, trying to disguise my condition. I knew full well why the cleric had taken it upon himself to come to the house.

'Señora Weiss,' he said, wrinkling his nose when I entered the room, as if he was speaking to a woman of loose morals. He remained seated on our new, red, satin-covered sofa, with his hat on the French mahogany table I had recently persuaded Francisco to purchase. I did not sit down, but stood just inside the door.

'I have come to tell you that you must return at once to your husband. I have spoken to him and, out of charity, he is willing to accept as his own the child you are carrying. It is your Christian duty to return to him at once.'

I looked down at his portly form, sour face and curling lips, and, Isabel, I was furious. How dare this priest order me to go back to the man I despised.

'I shall stay where I am, Monsignor,' I said. 'I have made my decision. Please do not come here again. Furthermore, when you see Señor Weiss, you may tell him that neither his spies nor his threats have the least effect on me.'

He reacted as if he had been bitten by a rabid dog, jumped up, then leaned back on his heels and spat out at me.

'I will ask you once more, Señora Weiss. No, I will not ask. I command you to return immediately to your legitimate husband. You have caused sufficient scandal.'

I did not answer him and my silence seemed to madden him further. He lurched towards me, his finger wagging in my face, spittle foaming on his thick lips.

'If you do not do as I say this very day, I forbid you ever to enter my church, or any other church in Madrid, or in all Spain. You will be excommunicated, do you hear? Excommunicated. You are putting your soul in danger. You will roast in hellfire. You will be damned.'

You look shocked, Isabel, but I was not frightened. My immortal soul is my own business.

'Please leave this house at once,' I said to that monsignor, calm as could be. I believe I may even have said *my house*. And though he blustered some more and wagged his fat finger at me, he left in a whirl of black cape and sour breath. After he had gone, I have to admit, I had a few moments of doubt about the course I had taken, but my third child was due shortly and I had enough to contend with. Isidoro continued making threats against me. I am quite sure that if it had not been for Francisco's position at Court and in society, he might have succeeded in carrying them out.

Besides all this, Isabel, I had to suffer living in a house impregnated with the spirit of Doña Josefa. I had to endure the sight of her dresses hanging still in the closets and her shoes lined up in the cabinet. Would you believe, Isabel, that her portrait used to hang above our bed? Francisco would not hear of anything of hers being removed. It was like living inside someone else's skin. Like being a parasite.

There was one really magnificent dress in the closet, covered in gold and silver embroidery, a wonderful garment; it must have cost thousands of reales. I was trying it on one day, after Rosario was born, though it was much too large for me, and was admiring myself in the mirror when Francisco came into the room. He almost tore it off me, shouting, 'That dress was a gift to my wife from the Infante, Don Luis. You are never to touch it again. Never!'

Now you see what I had to endure, Isabel. You may think I was lucky to have lived in fine houses with servants and to have myself and my children supported by Francisco but it was not a bed of roses to have been in such an invidious position, living as Francisco's de facto wife. Shunned by society. Duchesses may do as they please in this country, but we mere mortals are expected to conform.

And then there was Javier. Although at first he seemed to accept me as Francisco's companion, and indeed once declared that he was glad to see his father happy again, I was not deceived for an instant. I was twenty-five at the time and he was three years older. Although he had already been married to Gumersinda for seven years or so and had a six-year-old son, I knew right well what he was thinking when he looked at me. I have seen that look in men's eyes all my life. *I'll have to take care here*, I said to myself. *Cousin Gumersinda would scratch out my eyes.*

But when Rosario was born, Javier turned against me and would accept neither of us. He has made my life a misery since then. All these years I have had to suffer his arrogance and disrespect. He tried to poison his father against me, telling him that I had many lovers. Worst of all, he made up a vile story that Rosario was the child of a certain Señor Hoogen, an ancient German merchant, who was a friend of Isidoro's *father*, for God's sake.

You know, Isabel, I am quite convinced that Javier – his precious Javier – is the reason why for so many years Francisco refused all my pleas that he should legally adopt Rosario. Don Francisco de Goya, the fearless scourge of Spanish society, could not gainsay his son on any matter. He melted like ice in August when that spoiled wastrel wanted something. Do you know that when Javier married Gumersinda he gave them a house at Calle del los Reyes and made a pledge to support them and their future children and any servants they might have? *Virgen Santisima,* the foolish old man has already handed over to his darling Javier all his paintings, all our tables and the finest chairs and beds we had in Madrid, and so much else besides. Javier has never done a stroke of work in his life. He has none of his father's intelligence, talent or vivacity. He calls himself a painter but I have never seen anything of significance that he has produced. And he has produced precious little. Genius, it seems to me, is rarely inherited. I cannot think of any children of famous painters or writers who are worth anything, can you Isabel?

How I hated those five years I lived with Francisco in Madrid! I was a prisoner in a house dedicated to Doña Josefa's memory. My little Rosario had no companions – her half-brother Guillermo was five years older than her, and was not interested at all in his baby sister. Worst of all, as I told you, Francisco would not have me go out with him in society. He made excuses for not walking along the Prado with me on summer evenings, claiming he was too tired and too old. We could have gone in his carriage, of which he was so proud, but, according to him, that was not possible either, for one supposedly good reason or another. Oh, he made all manner of excuses, but I suspect that the truth is that he was not inclined to flout convention in this matter, although he had no difficulty flying in the face of convention when it suited him.

I had no choice but to stay at home with my children. Whenever I went out to the shops to console myself with the purchase of a new comb or a sandalwood fan, I had to endure insolent stares and loud whispers when I walked past with my daughter. Such things as: 'There she *goes,* Goya's *puta* with her little bastard. No wonder the Inquisition has seized and denounced those obscene images of her. They are a disgrace to Spain.'

The fishwives were wrong, of course. How could I have been the model for those paintings? I did not even know Francisco at the time. For God's sake, I was barely thirteen years old when those works were done for Godoy. The model was probably some *maja* or other; some say she was Pepita Tudó, one of Godoy's mistresses at the time. Others that it was the Duchess of Alba. But I cannot believe it was the latter as she must have been almost forty years old when those paintings were executed.

The naked one came back to haunt him during the Inquisition. Francisco was so worried at that dreadful period of our lives. Depressed too, much of the time. And when Señor de la Serna made that report on him, he really became quite disturbed. My dear friend, I shall never forget the day that he was summoned to appear before the Inquisition. Charges of obscenity were levelled against him – for that painting. Other charges too. About his loyalties. He rampaged around the house, breaking jugs and bowls, knocking over furniture, and using such foul language.

'How will you protect yourself now that Don Gaspar and your other influential friends are no longer in power?' I asked.

'Trust you, Leocadia, to remind me of the obstacles in my way,' he roared.

Quite unfairly I thought, because I was only pointing out the truth.

'What happened?' I asked when he returned from his interrogation. 'What did you say to them? Are we safe?'

'You need not worry,' he said. 'Luckily, they have not heard anything about *your* radical views. You are safe. I told them the truth about myself, which is that during the French occupation I kept myself shut up in my house and busied myself solely with my painting and engraving. I told them that I had ceased seeing those I formerly dealt with, because I hate the enemy who invaded our country. And I reminded them forcefully that I had gone to Saragossa after the siege and made enormous paintings celebrating the bravery of our people.'

I am not so sure that what he said was the whole truth, since it was well known that he had mixed with *afrancesados* such as Don Meléndez Valdés, who everyone knows believed that only the Emperor Napoleon could save Spain from misrule and repression. But I forbore to remind him of this fact.

'And what else did you tell them? Was that enough to set you free?'

'Well, I had some more persuading to do. I convinced them that I had wanted to flee Spain to escape from the French, but was prevented by the threat that all my possessions would be confiscated. I also informed them that I had refused to draw a salary from the French, which has resulted in my impoverishment. I told them that my family and I had survived only because I sold all my jewellery. So they had enough proof of my innocence and I am a free man. Free, but exhausted.'

Francisco could be most persuasive when he set his mind to it. It cannot have been easy to convince those Inquisitors of his innocence in the face of evidence to the contrary which was common knowledge. Perhaps his status of Court Painter saved him.

They did not persecute him further. I can tell you I was very much relieved, especially when he said they had not heard any of my views on the state of our country and on who was responsible. I have learned to keep my opinions to myself since then. Not that his intellectual friends ever listened to women.

My goodness, eleven o'clock already! Time for *onces*. I am quite hungry. Are you, Isabel? All this talking we're doing! Let's have it here in my room by ourselves. I'll tell Rosario to eat in the kitchen with the maid. There is still so much we have to discuss.

I tried to interest myself in Francisco's work, but he wanted no discussions with me about his art. When he was painting, he was a different man, not the one who was ill quite often and who worried about money. There were many Goyas. Only occasionally did he make comments about his clients.

'That English duke is a vain peacock, wanting all his stupid medals painted on his jacket in the correct order and type,' he complained of the Duke of Wellington.

They did not get on well together those two. The Duke hated the portrait.

'It's a caricature,' he shouted. 'You have made a mockery of me, Señor.'

Francisco replied, 'I regret that you do not like yourself. I flatter nobody.'

Isn't it strange, Isabel, how the very person who receives adulation one minute is reviled and spat upon in the next? Do you remember the time when we Spaniards could not praise the Duke of Wellington highly enough? He was given an estate near Granada and so many honours, but when his troops destroyed San Sebastian there were cartoons of him in all the newspapers, and the scandals of his womanising washed away his great military reputation. Remember, too, how we praised Napoleon when he first came to Spain, how we saw him as our saviour. Remember how we greeted the butcher Murat with great delight.

I had been married to Isidoro for about a year when the French forced our Royal Family to leave Madrid and held them captive at Bayonne. You were in Madrid then, Isabel weren't you? Do you recall what you were doing that day in May, twenty years ago now, when we Madrilènes rose up against Napoleon, and in retaliation Murat attempted to massacre us all? Had I not been pregnant with my first child, I would most certainly have gone out into the streets and pulled a red-coated Mameluke off his horse, and spat on those who would enslave us Spaniards. Isidoro, coward that he was, shut us into the house and forbade me to throw sacks of pepper, or furniture, or flowerpots, or anything at those vile French soldiers. I rejoiced when I heard that the General of the Imperial Guard had been killed when a woman had hurled a flowerpot down on his head from her balcony. How I wish I had been that woman.

Isidoro would not allow me to go out for a week, so I saw nothing of the dreadful events. Francisco told me that he was visiting Javier, who lived near Puerto del Sol at the time, and that he had heard that the first Mameluke had been killed by a shot from the nearby house of Don Gabriel Bález, a relation of Gumersinda. He also said that he watched the shootings at Montaňa del Princípe Pío through a telescope and that he later went out at night to make sketches of the corpses. Artists are so gruesome, aren't they?

Have you seen the two enormous and magnificent paintings Francisco made about those bloody events? It was not until years later that he got financial support from the provisional government to commemorate the bravery of the Madrilènes on the second and third of May in 1808. Do you know how long he had to complete them? Two months! The man worked night and day. I thought he would collapse from exhaustion but he seemed to gain even more energy from the work. It was as if the bravery of the men being shot was injecting Francisco with extra strength. Those are my favourite of all Francisco's works, and I hope that in future years these paintings will be what he is remembered for.

Do have some more *huevos estrellados*, my dear. Or a *tortilla guisida?* They really are very good. I insisted that we bring a Spanish cook with us here. French cuisine is all very well, but it's not like ours, is it? In exile, one needs as many reminders of home as possible. Where was I? The dreadful events of May 1808 in Madrid. Well, we have had enough of that, haven't we? All that was before I met Francisco, six years before I gave him Rosario.

He was terrified that she might not survive. One night I awoke and found him gone from our bed. Where did I find him only in the nursery watching over her cradle like a nurse!

'You'll kill yourself,' I reprimanded him, 'if you don't sleep after all the work you've done today. You forget that you are almost seventy.'

But he turned away from me and continued his watch over our child.

She was the only one he would tolerate in his studio while he was working. When I used to try to take her away, he would smile and say, 'Leave her with me. She has the soul of an artist, and so she cannot disturb me.' He even allowed her to help him with his lithographs, and taught her to mix colours. They were like twin souls, those two, always chatting and laughing together.

'Remind me of the sound the rain makes in the olive trees. Describe the sound of the water in the fountain. Tell me what you can hear around us now.'

Those were the kinds of impossible demands he made of me. He needed to rid himself, he said, of the maddening noises in his head by trying to remember ordinary sounds. And once he asked me, 'What does your voice sound like? And Rosario's laughter?'

As if anyone could answer such questions!

I had to learn to speak only when he could see my lips. He did not always understand what I was saying, being too impatient to wait until I had finished, and jumping to conclusions and getting hold of the wrong end of the stick entirely. I did not find it easy to communicate with him, I have to admit, and often when the frustration became too much for me, I would simply not speak to him for days. He would be cold and bitter towards me then, which would lead to arguments between us. As the years went on, however, and he grew older and frailer, we squabbled less. He did not seem to care what I did or whether I spoke to him or not. Rosario, however, communicated effortlessly with her father, and he with her.

You know, he was so stubborn that it took me five years to persuade him to leave Madrid. I found the atmosphere of repression, the tales of the tortures of the Inquisition and the persecution of my liberal friends too much to cope with. I was also afraid for Francisco, for both of us, and I thought it better if we lived quietly in the countryside. He was becoming more and more strange and secretive, obsessive with carnivals, masks and witchcraft. The work I saw in his studio (I went in there when he was out of the house) was savage and grotesque. He had made puddles of colour, then scribbled over them, smudged them until weird shapes emerged. I feared for his sanity. I worried that he might antagonise those in power. It was better for us to be out of Madrid.

I found the ideal place, just beyond the Segovia Bridge, near San Isidro. He paid sixty thousand reales for it, quite a good price in 1819, for such a fine house and land. He painted me on the wall, asked me to wear my black dress and to lean against the mantelpiece. I do not care for that painting. I look too sad and, besides, it is placed right opposite the monster Saturn. He did another one of me – thankfully not on the monster walls – in which I am reading a letter. That is much more like me as I was then.

When he was not covering the rooms with witches and hobgoblins, or playing with Rosario, Francisco was working in the garden at La Quinta. He extended it, had a house built for the gardener, a new drainage system installed, and extensive vineyards planted. He was obsessed with that garden. Working and walking in it seemed to bring out a different side of him – more gentle, less hurried, and a good deal less concerned about money.

Such a difficult time we had four years ago. When King Ferdinand was restored to power, we were in a panic and we had to flee La Quinta in a great hurry. Such an upheaval! My dear friend Don Tiburicio most graciously accepted to look after Rosario and Guillermo for me, while Don José de Duas y Latre sheltered Francisco. We made our separate ways to France.

What a relief it was when the King pardoned Francisco. Do you know what he said?

You have deserved exile, you have merited the garrotte, but you are a great artist and we will forget everything.

Artists, as I have said, are not to be treated like other men. The King then gave Francisco permission to retire and granted him a pension sufficient for us to live comfortably here in Bordeaux. Not that his pension meant that Francisco ever stopped working every hour he could. This convinced me that he did not work for money. I'll show you some of his last works – miniatures made in ivory – strange works; strange, like almost everything that interested the man.

I looked after him well through all his illnesses and nobody can say to the contrary. It was *me* who was beside his bedside day and night, nursing and humouring him, *not* cousin Gumersinda, or his precious son. Rosario delighted him and made his last years a pleasure, but now what is to become of us both? We shall be at the mercy of Javier and Mariano unless Francisco has made provision for us. I pray God that he has.

4

JOSEFA
MADRID, 1 JUNE 1812

No! This is not how I would have wished to leave this life. Despite my desertion of Him, I had hoped God would have had mercy on me. Why can He not grant me reconciliation, allow me a little final peace? Why am I still tormented? If suffering is His price, surely I have suffered enough to merit some degree of ease before I die? Could He not, even at this late hour, afford me some understanding of why my life with you, Francisco, has been so difficult?

'This is Francisco Goya,' my brother Francisco said, 'from Fuendetodos. He intends to be the greatest painter in Spain.'

My brother laughed when he said that. He was already a well-known artist in Aragon and a member of the Madrid Academy. And you were a poor, ill-educated nobody. Perhaps he was amused by your arrogance. My sisters and I were sitting by the window making lace. I looked up to examine the man who would be the greatest painter in Spain and was surprised. You were unlike any of my brother's acquaintances; so awkward-looking and uncouth, a short fellow with thick, wild, black curls, wearing a poorly cut jacket and battered boots. But you stood there in our salon like a young bull in the arena, full of pent-up energy, and giving off a powerful sense of belief in your own prowess. You had the most piercing dark eyes I had ever seen. You still have that look in your eyes, Francisco.

Although you nodded and bowed towards us young women, I knew you were not taking any notice of us. You had come to talk to my brothers about painting. *A rather bumptious, rough-looking fellow, with notions beyond his station*, I said to myself, and I went back to my lace. So why did I adjust my position so that my ringlets fell over my cheek, and rearrange the sash on my sky-blue dress? Why, on the following day, did I ask my brother about you as casually as I could, as if you were of no real concern to me?

'As you saw, he's a very ambitious fellow,' he answered. 'He has already entered the Madrid Academy competitions. Although I would have liked to have voted for a fellow Aragonese, I could not because his work lacks refinement and finish. I have heard that he feels aggrieved because, for some reason, he expected to have my support. As you know, our brother Ramon was judged to be the winner. No doubt that rankles with young Goya.'

He was right, wasn't he, my brother? It rankled with you, and no matter what successes you have had since then, you could never let go of those early rejections. You must open up old wounds and pick at them. Is that what fuels your ambition? Is that why you betrayed my brother?

Ah, why am I exhausting myself now? I have so little time left before I go to whatever reward or punishment I am due; it would be better if I repaired my soul. But I cannot dictate what drifts into my mind. I am too worn-out and too ill to make choices.

Are you over there by the window, Francisco? Sometimes I am sure that I can see you sitting in that high oak chair, with your back to the wall and your face turned towards me in the gloom. But there are more times when I do not sense your presence; times when I am conscious only of my own wasted body and my wandering mind.

You came often to our house. All my brothers, Ramon, Francisco, and Manuel befriended you and treated you so well. My dear brother Francisco, God rest his soul, lent you money and did everything he could to help you when he first met you. Then you disappeared and Francisco told me that you had gone to study painting in Rome. 'He's a wild fellow,' my brother said. 'There are all sorts of rumours about him.'

About a year later I was in the garden watering my roses when Ramon came through the courtyard with another man. 'Josefa,' he called, 'do you remember Francisco Goya? Well, here he is, newly arrived from his triumphs in Italy.'

'The man from Fuendetedos?' I said, surprised to find myself wishing I was not wearing my old green dress. You looked splendid in a silk shirt and an elegant Italian embroidered jacket with a crimson border. Although your cheeks were still chubby and high-coloured like a peasant, your mouth stubborn and your eyes rebellious, there was a new air of sophistication about you, as if Italy had rubbed smooth some of your awkward angles, and fashioned a gentleman of sorts.

One Sunday after Mass, my brother came to me in the kitchen and asked: 'How do you find Francisco Goya since his return from Italy? Do you think him different in any way?'

Wondering what this was leading to, I replied: 'Yes, he seems to have changed, but I have not spoken often enough to him to have formed a proper opinion.'

'He's making quite a name for himself. He was very successful, it seems, in Italy and now he has been commissioned to paint the *coreto* in El Pilar. I believe that, with my help, he can make a reasonable living as a painter, and I am inclined to think, therefore, that he would make a suitable husband for you. You are twenty-six, Josefa, and it is high time you married. What do you think? Would you accept Francisco Goya?'

'Has he asked you for my hand?' I was annoyed with myself for blushing.

'He would like one of you girls, and since you are the eldest, it is only fair that it should be you,' my brother said with the air of a man who had a lot on his mind, and settling his old-maid sister would relieve some of his burden.

What choice did I have? If my brother, who had looked after us since our parents died, was satisfied that this Francisco Goya was a suitable match, despite the facts that his father was a poor gilder, that he had little formal education, was rough-spoken, had no income to speak of nor private means or status, then I supposed I must accept his judgement.

'As you wish, brother,' I said. 'I'll marry Francisco Goya from Fuendetodos.'

You never tried to court me, wrote me no love notes, carried no flowers for me to our house, nor did you buy me fine combs. I knew full well that you wanted to marry me for the Bayeu name and influence, and yet there was an intensity about you, an energy and a passion that was compelling. *Life with such a man*, I thought, *could never be dull*. Even a docile young woman like me, who was not very pretty or rich, longed for passion and excitement.

Our wedding day – 23 July 1773, in the cathedral of El Pilar. Your fresco in the *coreto* gleamed fresh and wonderful. I took that as an omen and I was happy.

I had so few expectations: only that my husband would provide for me and for whatever children God might bless us with; only that my husband would honour me and my family.

It was not your fault that you were poor, that we had to depend on my brother Francisco's charity to support us. We were happy enough at first, weren't we? Until the babies came.

All lost. Taken from me one by one. All except Javier, our dear little Javier. Seven babies. Year after year bearing and burying another child.

We had been married one year when Antonio Juan Ramon, our first son, was born. You were so pleased to have a boy. 'We'll have a feast to celebrate the birth of our son,' you declared, despite the fact that we had so little money. I was happy also, but too ill to make preparations.

There was no feast. Antonio lay dead in his cradle in the morning. Why did God do this to us? Why did He snuff out a little life so callously?

Esebio Ramon, our second son, was born here in Madrid. He was a bigger baby and stronger than Antonio. 'There will be no talk of a feast,' I said. 'We shall not tempt God.' No matter. The child did not survive the winter.

I was stricken with a sickness of mind and body worse than the plague. There was no hope, no reason for me to go on breathing. I lay in my separate bed like an empty jug, cracked and useless. You were patient for a while, but you could not stay away from my bed for too long, and barely one year later I was unbearably with child again.

Vicente Anastasio was born. And died after a few weeks. Three fine sons for the grave.

'I tell you, Francisco, we are cursed. No more children. I will bear no more sacrifices for a cruel God.'

You raged and sulked when I would not lie with you. You said it was unnatural for a man and wife not to lie together; claimed that a man needed sexual congress to remain strong and healthy. What did you care for a woman's health? Making me pregnant every year, forcing me to carry babies who died before their eyes changed colour. Was that healthy? Was that natural?

Am I being unfair to you? I know how you longed for a son, or even a daughter. That night after Vincente died, I heard you weeping behind the closed door of your studio.

'We'll call her Maria Pilar Dionisia, our first daughter. Pray God she is stronger than her brothers. She's plumper and more solid. She has rosy cheeks and dark curls like her father. Six weeks and thriving. God is good, after all.'

The dark clouds lifted from me and hope poured into my heart like sunshine.

'I will sew such wonderful dresses for this child. She will be a solace to us in our old age. Just look at her dimples, Francisco. Is she not beautiful? We are truly blessed, at last.'

The eve of Christmas. Maria Pilar looked a little flushed. She coughed all night long. With each cough, my heart almost stopped. The doctor came and did his best, but by the feast of Saint Nicholas our daughter had grown grey and hollow-chested, like a husk. I dragged myself to the convent of Las Calatravas to ask the sisters to say novenas for her. We offered Masses, lit candles, abstained from meat, we implored God to save her.

He answered our prayers and our child revived. I thought my heart would burst with gratitude. I gave my pearl necklace to the sisters at Las Calatravas.

We should have stayed with her all night. We might have saved her. She died without a whimper in her cradle and we found her as stiff and cold as pity in the morning.

'Pepa, my dearest wife, you must eat something,' you scolded me; 'and you cannot stay in the dark with the shutters closed all day long.'

'I have no will to live. I cannot eat a morsel. Sleep evades me. I long only to join my dead babies. I am a healthy woman, Francisco, not too old, yet all my children die before they can hold their heads up straight. I cannot keep them alive. If this is the will of God, I do not want to know Him. He has no pity.'

You had no pity either. 'I cannot bear any more children,' I told you over and over. 'It will kill me.'

But you refused to leave my bed. For this I hated you. I hated God. I hated life.

Our son Francisco was born in 1780, in high summer – August, the month you began to work with my brother on the frescoes in El Pilar. You were elected to the Royal Academy and were so pleased with yourself.

'A new son, and proper recognition of my talents,' you boasted.

I was beyond caring. 'Have you no eyes for anything except your paintings? Do you not notice your wife's distress, husband? Do you not know that there is no christening robe for Francisco? I burned it when Maria Pilar died. The new child will get no breast milk from me, nor will I go into the nursery to see if it lives or dies.'

For I knew in my bones that it would die, cursed like all the rest. No doctor could explain why these perfectly formed creatures did not survive longer than a few months. *Nobody* could tell me why. There was nothing in my family which predicted it, nothing in yours that I knew of. Was my milk poisoned? But I did not breastfeed little Francisco. Was the midwife to blame? Not that either. I employed a different one for each of the births, just in case. I could find no reason, other than the wrath of God. He took all my babies. He did not permit one of them to live long enough to say 'Mama' or even 'Papa.' Why?

I looked after my babies so well. We were not poor, uneducated peasants living in a dirty cottage. I watched over their cradles far into the night, kept them warm or cool according to the season of their birth, prayed over them. So why did God allow such repeated tragedies to befall us? Santa Maria would never permit a mother to suffer like that. She could not do such a thing because she knew the pain of seeing her own – her only – son dying. It was He, God the Father, who allowed the torture and the crucifixion of His own son. No wonder, therefore, that He allowed our children to die. For He is the cruel god of sacrifice.

I was thirty-two years old; my sixth baby had just died. Five born, one dead in the womb. Wise creature, it spared itself the futility of being born. When I knew it was no longer alive, I was pleased. Yes, pleased, may God forgive me. Why did He not take me too? I would gladly have left this cruel world.

Now I am near death. I pray for it to come and release me so that I can lie with my baby, Hermengilda, with all my babies, in the tomb. God take me now. For I can suffer no more.

Are you there, Francisco? I cannot see you in the dark. Can you hear me? *Hear* me! Santa Maria! I must be delirious. What sins did you or I commit to deserve such punishments?

Ah, I can hear you now. My dear, you are sobbing. The darkness must be in my head, for you have been reading my lips. My eyes are too heavy to open, even to look at you. I am sorry for bringing back all this grief to you. No, that is not the truth. I am not sorry. What saddens me is that I have not spoken to you of these things before now.

I never even allowed myself to say this aloud, but the truth is that when Hermengilda died, three weeks after she was born, I turned away from God in my heart and soul. Our lives are as meaningless to God as those of the animals. Cats and dogs die without reason. We are no different. We fool ourselves if we think otherwise. There is no kind-hearted, fatherly God watching over us. Santa Maria, she cares about us, but since she could not save her own son, she is powerless to help us. All she can do is comfort us in our sorrows. *Santa Maria, Mater Dei, ora pro nobis.* She prays for us sinners now and at the hour of our death. Santa Maria, pray for this dying sinner, I beg you.

'Let us hope this one will get a chance to grow,' you said when Javier was born.

What foolishness! God had abandoned us. Why could you not see that?

'He will die like his brothers and sisters,' I told you. 'Why even bother to name the child? How can you trust such a treacherous God? How can you paint pink-faced, chubby children for the royal dining room in the palace of El Pardo while your own infants are crying weakly in their cribs? How can you bring yourself to depict happy children enjoying the bright pleasures of the countryside while our children die in their cradles in dark rooms?'

You made no reply. Men are made differently from women. They are not connected.

Miracle of miracles, Javier survived. I could not believe it when he reached his first birthday, when he started to walk and when he uttered the word I thought I would never hear, *Mama*, I felt as if my heart would break with joy.

You became obsessed with money; making it, investing it, spending it, and you are equally obsessed with the fear of losing it. All those letters you wrote to Don Martin seeking his advice about good investments. Sometimes I suspect that you care more for money and position than for your painting. You are so suspicious of those you see as your rivals, convinced they are plotting against you at every corner. You're determined to be the most important, which means, for you, the wealthiest, artist in Spain. Am I right in judging you so?

But you were never miserly, Francisco. That is not one of your faults. You provide handsomely for the running of this house. You supported your mother until she died and you continue to support your sisters and older brother. You allowed me to purchase the white satin bed mattresses I longed for, as well as the Indian nankeen hangings with the arabesques of purple wool, which I wanted for the salon. You clothe me in the most elegant dresses; buy exquisite fans and combs for me, in which I have not the slightest interest. We have servants, fine furniture and a carriage. We can eat as much *pan candeal* as we wish and have partridge for *las onces* whenever we like. And you make no objection when I spend thousands of reales on presents to send to my family in Saragossa.

'Let them see that Don Francisco de Goya is a man of substance,' you say.

You turned out to be a devoted father to our only child. Fussed like an old grandmother over his health. No breeze was allowed to blow on your little Javier. The slightest chill sent you running for the best doctors in Madrid. You instructed our cook to make special dishes for your son and you went to the great expense of employing a nurse to sit by his cot through the night until the child was four years old.

The first thing you did when you came into the house was to bound up the stairs to Javier. The poor little fellow was not allowed to play with other children in case he caught an illness. You forbade me to go near him if I had the slightest fever or headache. If anything had happened to that boy, you would have pulled Heaven down to Hell. You would have threatened God and all his archangels.

Please do not fuss over me. I do wish you would stop trying to feed me, to make me sit up and take medicine. No medicine can save me, and I do not wish to eat. For I do not want to live another day. I was ready to die years ago, yet I have lived on unwillingly to be an old woman of sixty-five. I am not like you, Francisco; you will live until you are a hundred. I do not think you will ever be ready to die.

It is blessedly cool in this room now. At last I am beginning to feel some peace. The strange thing is that all this talking seems to be calming me. In all our years as husband and wife we have not had much time for such talk, have we? You were so rarely at home. And when you were here, you were always too busy in your studio to talk or to listen to your wife. Of course, I understand that, as Court Painter, there were a great many demands on your time and energy. Even so, you rarely chose to spend what free time you had at home – preferring to go to the *corrida*, or to hunt, to attend *tertulias*, the theatre, or indeed to be anywhere except here.

You chose to leave me alone in Madrid with little Javier while you spent months on end with that licentious widow in Cadiz. That is hard to forget. Or to forgive.

Enough. I will sleep some now. You may go. Perhaps I will speak again when I wake. I hope you will come back and listen to me. Surely that is not too much to ask, husband, after almost forty years of marriage?

You came raging into the room like a demented bull.

'Those canons at El Pilar think they can treat me like an apprentice,' you roared. 'Who do they think I am? How dare your brother correct my work? Just because he obtained the commission for me, he thinks he can supervise and judge me, that he can inform Canon Allué that my work is not good enough because I refuse to make the corrections he, the great Bayeu, requires of me! I will not have your brother, or that arrogant canon, or anyone else tell me that there are defects in my frescos, that Charity is not *as decent as she should be*. Nor will I listen to rebukes that I should be more appreciative of my brother-in-law. And I most certainly will not be told that my sketches for the pendentives are *unfinished*, or faulty in any way.'

Why did you inflict this on me, knowing that I was pregnant once more? Had you no compassion? You ranted on and on.

'That dome is twenty-eight metres from the ground, so how could Canon Allué or the public see what he claims are *mistakes in the colours, attitudes and arrangements of the drapery*? Allué also has the audacity to say that the background is *too dark and lacking in detail*! Francisco Bayeu is the one who is behind this, make no mistake. I will not be persecuted in this manner. I refuse to produce sketches like an apprentice, or to have them corrected by one who paints domes as if they were flat canvases on an easel.'

'Calm yourself. You will have a seizure if you continue like this. And please remember that you are speaking about my brother, who has supported us and promoted you, and without whom you would not have this commission.'

'I have worked harder and faster than anyone else on that dome, two hundred and twelve metres of fresco to paint and *I* have almost finished, while *others* are still only beginning. I intend to take this matter further, Pepa. I shall go to the Cathedral Commissioners. I shall inform them that an artist is not a tradesman; an artist must have artistic freedom.'

So you went to the Commissioners and you denounced my brother. You told them that you refused to comply with his corrections. You put my brother in a dreadful situation. You showed yourself to be an ingrate. Francisco had agreed to decorate the chapel on condition that you were employed as his assistant. Surely he had every right to supervise the work? How could you imply that my brother was acting against you?

He protected your interests by complaining to the authorities that you and Ramon were expected to do too much work for too little money, didn't he? Did that not show that my brother respected and valued you? Why couldn't you accept that *he* was the one responsible; why couldn't you have allowed him to ensure that all the work complied with the same rules or standards to achieve the same style? Why did you have to be so ungrateful, after all my brother had done for us – for you. Francisco was an important and influential master, and yet he promoted you, an obscure provincial. Why did you put such a prestigious commission in jeopardy?'

'I forbid you to contact your jealous brother, do you hear?' you roared at me and your eyes were like fire. 'I am your husband, your loyalty is to *me* now, *not* to the Bayeus.'

You shut yourself up in your studio all day and would speak to no one. You left me isolated in that draughty house while you raged about in your room, striking the furniture with your cane. And when the letter was finished, you subjected me to your crazed reading of it, taking no regard of my poor health.

I am the victim of a vicious slander, the target of malevolent prejudice which has its roots in the artistic jealousy of Don Francisco Bayeu, who has complained to the cathedral chapter about my work. I will not have my reputation as a painter tarnished by such slanderous attacks, and I maintain that the frescoes I have made are of the highest quality and require no adjustments whatsoever. Nor will I make any corrections.

My brother jealous of you! He was considered one of Spain's best painters, he was Mengs' assistant, he was a member of the Academy of San Fernando when you were a nobody. He *made* you.

Felix Salcedo, one of my brother Manuel's fellow monks, wrote to you in an attempt to restore calm and make you see reason when the scandal became the talk of Saragossa.

Don Francisco Bayeu is the premier artist of the day and on the verge of becoming first painter to the king. You may be a talented artist, but you are a novice who has yet to establish a reputation. Pray do not pick a fight with the entire cathedral chapter. Please allow Francisco Bayeu to exercise the responsibility which is rightly his.

Finally, you saw sense. You promised to write to the Commissioners saying that you would agree to work under my brother's supervision. I was so happy for I hate conflicts of any kind and I was greatly relieved that I could visit my family again. But that was not to happen.

Why did you not act on those good intentions of yours? Why did you finish the dome with such bad grace? And why did you fly into another tantrum when you went to see Canon Allué to collect the remaining forty-five thousand reales for the commission? Above all, why did you force me to leave Saragossa so suddenly, before I had time to see my family? That was so cruel. I had no quarrel with them. A wife is expected to take her husband's side, but in my heart I agreed with my brother Manuel. Like him, I loved you, but as he put it, not *in defiance of truth, reason and the interests of my own brothers.* How I have always hated to hear you saying: *The memory of Saragossa and the painting burns me alive.* I am the one who is burned alive. Every day. And you are the cause of the fire.

'Javier will be our last child.' Do you remember me saying that to you on the day our son was baptised? I swore to God I would never lie with you again. You had estranged me from my family. You had dishonoured the Bayeu name. I withdrew my affection from you. You might carry on your affairs with *majas* or countesses all you wished. I knew what was going on. Although I was not one to parade in the evenings on the Prado, or to listen to tittle-tattle, servants gossip and neighbours and relatives speak volumes in their avoiding eyes and pitying glances.

After we moved to Madrid, you worked like a demented person. You were so determined to be a success, to survive without my brother's financial or professional assistance. Sometimes, if little Javier woke and I had to fetch him some milk from the kitchen, I passed your studio and saw the gleam of light from under the door at three or four in the morning.

'Count Floridablanca wants his likeness done by me!'
'And who is Floridablanca?'
You were standing in the doorway, your face red with running from your meeting with him, your eyes wild with victory, and you looked at me as if I was an ignorant woman from a mountain village.
'My dear Pepa, do you not know that the Count of Floridablanca is the Minister of the Interior for King Charles and is, therefore, one of the most important men in Spain? He has promised that he will do whatever he can for me.'
You looked extremely satisfied with yourself, but I could not fully share your pleasure. Your ambition always struck me as too worldly, too self-regarding. Oh, that is unfair of me. I know that you had to struggle to obtain commissions. Forgive me.

My head aches with so much talking. But what does a headache matter now? It will not kill me, nor will I live longer if I spend the time resting. I have to say a lot of things before I go. I was silent for too long. Is it not ironic that I turned against the fashionable world in which you sought to move at the same time that I had lost my faith in God? And is it not also ironic that, having lost my faith in God, I longed to live out my life in a secluded convent?

Like you, Francisco, I have learned much from observation. And from reflection. There is no meaning to many puzzles in this life, there are more puzzles than reasons. Our lives are held in a knot of opposites. By observing how you have succeeded in your ambition, I have learned that willpower, combined with luck and talent, can turn fortune's key. For myself, the 'timid little wife' of Don Francisco de Goya, I have learned also that those who sit quietly in a corner see much more of what is going on than those who mill in the crowd, chattering and preening themselves.

You have always stood both inside and outside the circle, haven't you? You were not dazzled out of your reason by the pomp and wealth of your surroundings when you were first patronised by the grandees. For the most part, you kept your native cynicism. In your work, you are not afraid to show society to itself in all its contradictions. That I did, and do still, admire about you.

It is dark again. Is it night? Are you still here? Can you lip-read in this gloom? Am I talking to myself? I am thirsty. I will drink a little water.

Thank you. I am glad that you are here. Tomorrow, perhaps, I will feel stronger and I will continue. It would greatly please me if you would at last spend some time with me before I die.

'I *told* you years ago in Saragossa that I would be the greatest artist in Spain, and I told your brother Francisco so. The Infante has commissioned me to paint his family.'

He seemed to be a kind man, Don Luis. What wonderful presents he sent me and Javier. The silver and gold gown he gave you for me that first time you went hunting with him at Arenas de San Pedro still hangs, hardly worn, in my closet, with the other fine dresses you bought me. I wore it once, I remember – the night you invited Don Gaspar de Jovellanos and Don Meléndez Valdés and some of your other grand intellectual friends and patrons to a *tertulia* at our house.

I was never at ease in such company. The conversations were of matters of which I had no understanding. And I was never clever at cards. I know it irritated you that I seldom wore any of those fine dresses or wished to attend *tertulias*. But I have always been a plain woman uninterested in fashion or show. You knew that when you married me. Besides, I could not bring myself to dress in fine clothes, and smile, and make inconsequential talk. I had no inclination to go out or to parade on the Prado. I desired nobody's pity or concern. I was used to my own company. You had become so busy with your commissions and your printmaking that, it seemed to me, you hardly noticed you had a wife. But you must have spoken kindly of me to your patrons.

'Look, Pepa, look what I have brought you from Chinchon. The Infante has sent you another present.'

Wrapped in pink silk, it was the most exquisite necklace of pearls and emeralds. Far too splendid for a dull woman like me who rarely went out.

The Duke of Altamura's little son, what was his name? Manuel Osorio? Yes, that was it. He was about the same age as Javier when you painted him. Bright scarlet suit with a gleaming gold sash. He was playing with a pet magpie, those malevolent cats waiting to pounce. You always loved children. That picture of the Osuna children with their parents and their toys. Your affection for them so clear in every brushstroke. You seem surprised that I am interested in your work. Why should you be? Two of my brothers were painters too.

'Pepa, Pepa, I have been made Court Painter. We're rich! Our future is assured. What would you like me to buy you? A new dress?'

You were always a connoisseur of women's clothes.

'What about a fine ivory fan? Or a French *armoire*? Whatever you want, my dearest wife, you shall have.'

You could be the most generous of men but I wanted nothing for myself. Perhaps I should have been more gracious. I sent presents to all my friends and relations in Saragossa while you bought yourself a gilded English carriage. Do you remember how it toppled over the first or second time you used it and almost killed somebody, so you had to get rid of it?

You purchased such splendid clothes with your new wealth. That is another side to you. You are a man of so many conflicting sides. The man who scorns grandees wants to possess fine clothes and carriages.

'I intend to start a *hidalgo* application. I will be *de Goya* from now on.'

A title too. Your mother would have approved; she never stopped talking about her *hidalgo* heritage.

'But, Francisco, don't you know that it is through my brother's agency that you've been appointed Court Painter?' You did not like me reminding you of his continued patronage, did you?

Maybe he will be content now. Perhaps he will control his tongue and his temper. That's what I told myself. But I was wrong. You are not a man to be content for long, are you?

I have tried to be a good a wife to you. I have never troubled you with my worries, have I, nor demanded any luxuries? Your food is prepared and cooked the way you wish, and there are no recriminations of any kind in our house. Is that not so?

Oh, though my head aches and my bones are deathly weary. I feel free at last, like a nun released from a contemplative order, allowed to make up for a lifetime's silence before she dies.

There were times, I remember, when we got on really well. When my dearest brother Francisco died you comforted me. You are capable of compassion, of tenderness even. And when your mother, the gentle Doña Gracia, went to her reward, you turned to me for comfort. That horrible year of 1789 when our little Javier had the pox we were united in our terror of losing him. I shall never forget those months. You were distraught, even neglecting your work to be with him. You wrote to your good old friend Don Martin that you had no life of your own for all that time, and that was the truth. But when Javier recovered, you went back to the glittering world you inhabited and I stayed at home with my child and my thoughts.

'There is someone of my profession,' you shouted, pushing aside the *olla podrida* I had asked Luisa to cook especially for you, 'who has told the King that I no longer wish to paint for his Majesty. And other contemptible people are inventing stories about me and telling his Majesty these lies.'

Here is what I said to myself when I heard that. *My husband sees conspiracies everywhere. He is insane. Don Martin will advise me. I will write to him this very night.*

'Since he was a youth, my friend Francisco has been of such a suspicious disposition. Do not worry, I am sure his present neurosis is a consequence of his being overtaxed by the demands of his position, as well as by the demands of his academic work. Indeed, he has told me as much himself. Have no fear, he will not go mad; he will deal with this through his work.'

That's what Don Martin wrote to me. The letter is in my writing box. You may read it after I am gone.

You produced more and more strange and hideous figures in your paintings, as if you wished to publicly mock your real or imagined detractors. You seemed to want to be independent, to be original, to escape the constraints of being Court Painter. At the same time you felt the need to change some of your habits, to become more respectable. You no longer went to hear *siguillollas* and *tiranes* because you needed to maintain *a certain dignity,* as you put it. You were never one to go in a straight line, were you, Francisco?

Don Martín was right. You did not go mad. But you worked yourself up into such a state that you became seriously ill and had to be granted leave by the King.

Our brother Ramon is dead, Manuel's letter said. I watched your face. You looked sad, but only for an instant, then your face hardened.

'He took Francisco's side against me in the El Pilar affair. We shall not attend his funeral.'

I hated you then. 'May God strike you down,' I shouted.

But still you refused to allow me to go to my brother's funeral.

On St. Joseph's Day I received God's response to my dreadful wish. You had disappeared from Madrid without any official permission. I had no idea where you had gone or why. I was used to your erratic behaviour and was not overly worried at first. As time went on, however, and there was no sign of you, I grew agitated and tried to trace you; to no avail. Then Don Sebastian Martinez wrote to me from Cadiz saying that you were with him.

He arrived at my house in a deplorable condition and he cannot go out. We must help him to recover, though I fear it will be a lengthy business. I have forbidden him to write to you himself, because I am afraid of the harm that would do his head, which is the source of his sickness. He has lost his eyesight and the noises in his head seem to have affected his hearing. I am sorry to tell you also, Doña Josefa, that he has lost his balance and seems most confused.

I had cast the evil eye on my husband and I was punished. You lay deaf, blind and bewildered far away in Cadiz. Every day Javier asked when his Papa was coming home. I lit candles, went each morning to the sisters at Las Calatravas. I promised God that I would go back to Him if he restored my husband to good health.

He is morbidly depressed, Don Martín wrote. *Such a genius as Francisco cannot live easily with the vanity and hypocrisy of this world. He sees too much, he feels too deeply, his nervous system is too sensitive, and it is this, in my opinion, which has made him ill. But fundamentally he is as strong as a bull and I am sure the waters at Trillo will effect his full recovery.'*

He was not completely correct, your wise friend. You stayed for months in Cadiz, recovered your eyesight and your balance, but when you came back to Madrid in the middle of 1793, you had not recovered all your senses.

A carriage pulled up outside our door and Javier and I rushed out to greet you. A shrivelled, bowed figure emerged. You looked like an oak tree that had been struck by lightning. I ran towards you, calling out your name. I was so pleased to see you alive that I did not care that you had abandoned us. You did not raise your head to look at me, nor did you answer me. 'Papa, Papa,' Javier shouted, his voice shrill with excitement. Still you did not raise your head to look at your wife and child. *The noises in his head have affected his hearing. Oh God, what have I done? My heart will crack. It is my fault. God is punishing me for my years of unwifely refusal. For my silences. For wishing him struck down.*

Sometimes I clamp my hands really hard over my ears, or stuff pieces of fabric into them, but I can still hear sounds, so I cannot imagine what is like to be completely deaf. Can you hear the sound of your own breath, I wonder? Which sounds do you miss most?

You never complained of your affliction. Your voice changed; became heavier, more emphatic, like the dead beat of a drum, and your eyes became more piercing than ever. Never very tolerant, you suffered fools less gladly, and your temper was even more volatile than before. Something else has changed in you also. It seemed to me that you had decided to stop pleasing your patrons, that you had determined to create whatever satisfied you. Deafness and suffering had, in a strange way, liberated you. Perhaps the hand of death allowed you to live as you wished. Just as it has allowed me to speak so freely to you now after my years of silence.

Francisco, I am heartily sorry. I am to blame for your deafness. It was God's punishment on me. But we go on because we have to. And then life changes.

After that illness, in my eyes you became vulnerable and therefore lovable once more. And although I admit that I found it disturbing that you brought more and more of the stupidities, the obscenities and the sadnesses of the world into your pictures, I also acknowledge that you tell the truth in your art. You are not afraid to show the dark side, even when you mix with those who live in bright splendour.

We go on and life changes. You were cursed with deafness, my affection and respect for you returned. And then *that woman* came to your studio. She had the arrogance to ask you to paint her face. Not her likeness, her face! As if you were a maid. I was passing outside the door of your studio. I heard her imperious command. I imagined you placing your hands on her aristocratic face and painting it with the sort of cosmetics used by *majas*. I was not amused.

I saw her arriving at our house. She swept up the stairs to your studio like a queen going to her private apartments. Later, I saw her leaving, with red bows in her hair, her cheeks rouged and powdered, a red sash tight around her tiny waist, her blackened eyebrows and kohled eyes, and her hair brazenly tumbling over her shoulders like a young girl's. You came out onto the street to help her into the waiting carriage. I was watching from Javier's bedroom window.

I knew from the outset that she was not going to be like any of the others. This affair would be different because I had grown to love you, but more than that, because this painted woman was no common little *maja,* but one of the wealthiest and certainly the most envied woman in Spain, more admired than the Queen herself. Even now, after all these years, although she is in her grave, may she rest in peace, it pains me to think of her.

What intrigues me is what she saw in you. You were a difficult, taciturn and deaf man of almost fifty. She was directly after the Queen in the hierarchy and you, despite your hidalgo pretensions, were lowborn. Were your strange paintings an aphrodisiac? Was that it? Perhaps her other lovers lacked your passionate sense of originality, your sweeping and indestructible ambition. Am I wrong in assuming that you were lovers? What was I to think?

'I have to leave Madrid for some months,' you announced.

When Javier, who was about twelve years old at the time, asked you why you had to go, and why you would not take us with you, your answer was that you had a very important commission to fulfil in Cadiz which would occupy all your time and energy.

And so you spent all those months in 1796 and '97 with the new widow on her estate at Sanlúcar de Barrameda. No doubt, you had plenty of time and opportunities there to paint her face again. And, no doubt, to paint her body in whatever indecent poses such a flirtatious woman would adopt.

Although I am quite certain that I will never be shown the sketches and paintings which I am sure consumed you for an entire time you spent there, I have my own imagination, Francisco. The thought of you with her in her apartments, in her gardens, tortured me. I hated her because I thought she had taken your affection, just when I had discovered my love for you, but my suffering had more cause than that. These last weeks, lying here on my deathbed, I have been puzzling why I suffered so much that spring.

I know now why I so disliked the Duchess of Alba. It was because she had the wealth, the opportunities, and the... daring, to live freely. Your duchess, Francisco, was free, while I, burdened with child-birth and child-death, by family background and convention, was imprisoned. I, plain timid Pepa, wife of the greatest artist in Spain who could not bask in his success, longed to be a different person. You have always been interested in contradictions, in reversals, haven't you? Well, she was my reverse; she was the other side of the coin I never spun. She was the choice I could never make; she lived as I could never dare. What I heard, and what I imagined, about her life, showed me the frustrations and limitations of my own. Compared to her, I was grit beside a diamond. And that is why I could never say her name. That is why my love for you darkened once more into withdrawal and silence. It was not fair, I know. You were not to know my fantasies. But what is fair in this life?

Among your *Caprichos,* the one you entitled *Sueño de la mentira y inconstancia*, you denounce her duplicity. But why expect women like her to be any more constant than men like you?

I have heard about many of the kind deeds she did, about the waifs and strays she gathered about her. May she rest in peace. Javier has shown me one of your portraits of her; the painting he tells me you kept for yourself, which you have promised to leave to him when you die. I have read your name on her ring. I have followed her pointing finger to the inscription *Solo Goya* in the sand at her feet. Sand shifts. It blows in your face. It blinds your eyes momentarily. It blows away.

5

JOSEFA
MADRID, 5 JUNE 1812

'Come nearer, child. Your grandmother will not eat you!'
'Why do you lie here all day with your eyes closed,
talking to yourself, Grandmamma?'

'Sit by my bed, Mariano, and I will tell you. No, first please
draw back the curtains so that I can see your face, and we can
talk in the light. That's better! Why do people think that the
sick require total darkness? Will we not be long enough in the
blackness of the tomb? Now, child, tell me how old you are.
Such a fine, big, strong boy. You must be at least seven. Eight?'

'I shall be six, Grandmamma, on my next birthday. Do
you not remember?'

'Six? Gracious me! Only six? And so tall and strong.
Old people forget, Mariano. We forget all sorts of things.
Important things, and not so important things.'

'But Grandpapa is older than you and he never forgets
anything.'

'The truth is that we are about the same age, child, but
you are right: Grandpapa never forgets anything.'

'Grandmamma, you said that you would tell me why you
lie here with your eyes closed, talking to yourself. I think you
forgot.'

'You know, you are just like your father, Mariano – always gently reprimanding me. I lie here because I am tired, and so ill that I can no longer get up. And my eyes are closed because I am remembering all the things that happened in my life and it is easier to do that with your eyes closed. Do you not close your eyes when you try to remember something? Of course you do! But why do you say that I talk to myself?'

'Because you do. Not *now*, Grandmamma; you're talking to me now. But when Papa and I came in, you were talking quite loudly and there was nobody in the room.'

'Where is your dear Papa? I do not see him.'

'I'm here, Mama, by the door. No, please do not try to sit up. I'm coming over.'

'Ah, Javier, my son, it does me good just to see your handsome face. Mariano was asking me why I was talking to myself. I had hoped your father was sitting with me. I thought I was talking to him. Where is he? Oh where is he? Why is he never with me?'

'Please, Mama, do not get so agitated. Papa is with the English duke, painting his portrait. He will come to see you as soon as he can.'

'The duke of this, the duke of that. Dukes, duchesses, kings and queens. He paints their likenesses, spends all his days with them and often his nights, too. He knows their characters. But even now your father has no time to spend with his wife. After almost forty years together, he does not know her. That is why I was talking, Javier. To make him know me before I die. But you tell me that he hasn't been here. I have been wasting my breath.'

'Mama, you are distressing yourself. Papa has to do his work. You know that. He comes to see you as often as he can. Were it in his power, he would stay with you all day, but he is overburdened with work.'

'Ah, Javier, Javier, when you were a child like Mariano here, you had a pox. Your father did not lift a brush for weeks; he would not leave your bedside. He even told the King about your illness. He stayed with *you* then.'

'Hush, Mama, hush now. Please do not cry. Mariano, go immediately to your mother; it's time for you to eat. Say goodbye to your grandmother. Give her a kiss. Yes, of course you may come to see her again.'

'Goodbye, child. Give a kiss to your mother for me. Tell her I remember the day she married your Papa. She looked so lovely. So young and sweet then.'

'You should try to sleep now, Mama; you have exhausted yourself. I shall leave you alone for a while.'

'Leave me? Why does everyone always want to leave? Why do you not want to *listen* to me? It is not as if I have spent my life talking. Or is it that you are afraid of what I might say? Is that it? Is it? Afraid I might finally ask some awkward questions? Or is your father the only one who is allowed to upset people? Because he is the great genius, the Court Painter, Don Francisco de Goya – so busy painting dukes that he cannot come to the bedside of his dying wife.'

'Mama, I beg you, stop. You are beside yourself. You will bring on another fit. So agitated, so, so …'

'Angry? Yes I am angry. I was too docile as a girl, too timid all my life. I have much to be angry about and I am ridding myself of it before I die. I will not carry poison with me into the next life. But all this does not concern you, my son. For you I have some last requests.'

'Whatever you ask, Mama. And I wish you wouldn't be angry.'

'There is the puzzle, Javier. Expressing anger dilutes it. Because it helps me to understand. So please do not try to stop

me; it does me good, you see. I want to die with as few sins as
possible on my soul. I need the great mercy of God. Sit nearer
to me, Javier. My voice is getting weak. There, that's better. I
can see your eyes now. Here, hold my hand.'

'Mama, you have no sins on your soul, I'm sure.'

'We all have sins, my son. But no more of that now. I feel
much more calm. I want to tell you something. When I die,
Javier, and that will be very soon, my estate will be divided
between your father and you. We made our wills last year.
He wants to be buried in Franciscan robes, to have Masses
and prayers said for his soul. Despite all the things he has said
about the Church, your father is a good Catholic at heart.
I need prayers and Masses too. He may deed some of his
property to you before he dies. He will most likely give some
of his paintings and prints into your safekeeping – life in this
country is so uncertain these days. Your Papa is well-known
and controversial and he has enemies. Now promise me this:
if there are any unseemly pictures among them – you know
what I mean, I'm sure – assure me that you will not show these
paintings in public. Promise me also that you will never sell
them. Will you do that for me?'

'Whatever you ask, I will do, Mama, to the best of my
ability.'

'Ah, Javier, always the diplomat. You will do what is most
opportune, won't you? No matter. I can only make a request; I
cannot bind you from the tomb. What I am going to ask you
now is not a request. This I *demand* that you do for me before
I die. Are you listening carefully? Don't squeeze my hand so
hard! Just hold it gently and look into my eyes. No, before I
begin, wet a cloth and cool my face. Plump my pillows, so
that I may sit up properly. Now, sit beside me again and I shall
tell you what I want.'

'I'm listening, Mama. But please do not exhaust yourself.'

'Javier, this is important. Many years ago, before you were born, my older brother Francisco was one of the most important painters in Aragon. Tio Francisco may have seemed a little austere, even somewhat brusque to you, but in truth he was the kindest of men. He helped your father greatly, as I have often told you. For instance, when he was awarded the commission to decorate the dome of El Pilar in Saragossa, he insisted that your father was given a contract as his assistant. Such an honour. The cathedral of El Pilar!

A glass of water, please. My mouth is dry. I am sorry to have to tell you this, my son, but it is time you knew. Your father repaid my brother's generosity by quarrelling with him publicly and by insulting the Canons of the Cathedral. He even threatened to leave Saragossa before his work in the Cathedral was finished. He forbade me to contact my family, forcing me to take his side against my own brother. That is one of the things I am still angry about. I lost years of my life to bitterness.

Tio Francisco paid for your father's studies in Italy. Did you know that? I thought not! I expect Papa told you he made his own way there, boasting that he had earned the money by joining a *cuadrilla* and fighting in *corridas* all through Spain. Not so, Tio Francisco paid for him to study in Rome, so that he might make something of himself, having failed in Spain. And indeed, thanks to my brother, Italy is where your father first gained the recognition that enabled him to progress so well afterwards in Spain.'

'Can you understand now why I am angry? You nod, Javier, but you do not fool your mother. You are your father's son. Tio Francisco died when you were about eleven. Your father and your uncle were reconciled eventually, thanks to my brother's efforts. Before he died, Francisco took the trouble to write to your father's old friend, Don Martin Zapater, seeking his intercession to make peace with your father. Don Martin showed me your father's letter of reply.

I greatly regret that relations between us have been strained and constantly pray God to rid me of the spirit of pride which always overwhelms me on such occasions. If I manage to observe moderation and do not fly into any more rages, my actions will be less evil for the rest of my days.

'I will say this much for your father: in his heart, he knows his faults, and sometimes even admits them. He painted a wonderful portrait of Tio Francisco and exhibited it at the Academy. But it is still difficult for me to find forgiveness in my heart for your father, for his years of hostility and ingratitude towards my brother, for his disrespect for the Bayeu name.

Now here is my command. You are to write to my last remaining brother, your Tio Manuel. You know he is still at the Monastery of Aula Dei. Write this very day. Ask him to come to Madrid to see me while I am still conscious. And after I am gone, you and he are to arrange for my burial in my family tomb in Saragossa. I have left instructions in the box in my closet over there which contains my will. This is my final wish, my son. Promise me that you will do this for me.'

'But you are not going to die, Mama. The doctors say there is not a great deal the matter with you. That you could get better, if you had the will to do so.

'I am going to die, my son. I do not want to live any longer. You are a strong, healthy young man; you have a wife to look after you, and a son to take your place. Your father has given you a grand big house and has ensured your pension from the King. You will all survive perfectly well without me.

Nobody here needs me any longer, and it is therefore time for me to go.'

'I wish you would not speak like this, Mama. We need you still. You are the heart of our family, please do not speak of dying.'

'A heart that has been broken, Javier, cannot go on beating. I am not saying that I am broken-hearted now, only that my heart has been broken so many times, it no longer has the power, or the will, to go on.'

'May I ask what else broke your heart, besides Papa's quarrel with Tio Francisco?'

'It is a great pity that you were not here earlier, Javier. I was talking about those things – about all your dead brothers and sisters; about things your father did which sorely grieved me. I am not sure if you know to what I am referring; I do not know what he has told you, man to man, about how he has lived his life …

I am too tired to talk any more. I will sleep now. Come to see me in the morning. Ask Gumersinda and Mariano to come with you one more time. And Javier, if your father comes home tonight, please tell him that I am waiting for him.'

6

JOSEFA MADRID, 10 JUNE 1812'

Saragossa. Four *toreros* enter the arena. Ramón smiles and waves up to me. Francisco, in orange breeches and a lemon shirt sashed in blue silk, his long hair gathered in a net, is letting the bull into the ring. Manuel looks tense and more than a little frightened. You, the matador, wearing the richest costume, salmon pink embroidered in gold, turn to face the bull, a scarlet *muleta* in your hand. Thundering hooves, snorting, the smell of bull on scattered dust, roars of the crowd, my heart banging against my bodice. Then... *viva,* your hat thrown to the ground, you advance to meet the bull's lowered head, raising high and thrusting your long sword into the beast's neck. And again. Dancing back from the spurting blood. *Viva! Viva!* You walk from the arena triumphantly, not a bloodstain on your white stockings.

Javier's fourth birthday. He is splendid in his new green suit with lace ruffles and gold sash, as splendid as the son of a duke. The two of you are sitting together, your head bent over him, the child looking up at you in wonder, listening to your stories about the Romero brothers, Pepe Hillo and

Costilliares. 'Pedro Romero killed five thousand, six hundred bulls in nearly thirty years in the *corrida*.' The child has no concept of such large numbers, but he is impressed by your solemn voice. 'And Pepe Hillo survived fifteen gorings before he finally died in the arena. I saw it happen, and it was one of the saddest days of my life.' Next you start complaining bitterly about Godoy banning the *corrida* as barbaric and unenlightened.

'What is barbaric, Papa?'

'Those who do not understand the *corrida*, son.'

'Do you understand the *corrida*, Mama?'

'Ask Papa about the French and the *corrida*.'

Bitterly estranged for years – those four young *toreros*. And me, poor Pepa, caught in the middle. Forced to side against my brother.

Valencia. Spring of 1789. The longest journey I ever made. You took me there to recuperate from another of my illnesses. We left Javier, aged five, at home with his nurse. Sweet days together. Too soon ended.

A fly is buzzing around my nose. Mosquitoes whine in my ear. Darkness. Heaviness. Heat. Still alive, then. Taking such an age to die. The lungs struggle against the will. Take me soon, Santa Maria. But first… forgive me, God.

The high-ceilinged rooms of my family home in Saragossa, tall windows looking over the courtyard. Mama's beloved roses. My childhood bedroom above the garden, the smell of orange blossom… the sound of my mother's singing. Sound of weeping all over the house when she left us orphans.

Papa, Mama, Francisco, Ramón, Rita, all my dead babies – I will see you all again very soon now. Manuel, please pray for me in your monastery. Pray that God and Francisco will forgive me before I die.

Bonaparte presenting you with the Royal Order of Spain, which you accept, bowing deeply, then back you go immediately to your studio to work day and night, engraving plates depicting the rape and murder committed by the French against our people. Contradictory Francisco. Who can know your motives?

You laud the bravery of Maria Augustin defending Saragossa against the French invaders. Then you paint a portrait of the usurping king, and carry out administrative work for the French. Contrary Francisco. You expose hypocrisy at the same time as you practise it. You deplore deception, and you deceive your wife. You claim to abhor vanity, and you order your boots from England, your *jabots* from France. You elevate your name to de Goya! You preach openness and honesty and you suspect your fellow artists of conspiring against you. Now kind, now brusque, now conforming, now dragged in front of the Inquisitors, now pleasing your patrons, now satirizing them in your prints, now querulous with adults, now infinitely patient with children. Infinitely contrary Francisco Goya.

Are you here, Francisco? What do you think of your wife's judgements? Am I being unfair to you? How do you reply? *Look at my work.* Is that all? Is that enough? Is there such a distance between life and art – between what you say you believe and how you act? Do artists – men of genius like you – have special dispensations to be perverse?

Plain as I am, in my bonnet and shawl. No flattery. The one painting you ever did of me. None either in the wedding miniatures of Javier and Gumersinda, their weak features shown as strongly as their good ones. Not king, or queen, or wife, or son is spared in your portraits.

You at twenty-seven, the year we married – a good likeness and not vain. At thirty-three, at your easel, plumper and more prosperous, your long hair tied back, white lace around your neck. Aged fifty, looking full at us, hair wild and loose, your black eyes staring, your mouth hard. The same year, the frontispiece for those infamous *Caprichos*, wearing a tall black hat, masterful in high shirt and frockcoat, your eyes as hard as olive stones, your big nose, your quarrelsome mouth.

But there is one flattering portrait; you standing sideways at your easel, beside a high window, wearing your tall hat, a fine, embroidered jacket, *jabot*, and silk stockings, much too young-looking for fifty. So, you see, you are not any freer from vanity than the rest of us ordinary mortals. You are stuffed full of inconsistencies, Don Francisco de Goya y Lucientes.

I wish people would leave me alone and let me live quietly, carrying out the work that I am obliged to do, and spending the remaining time on my own work. I do not want to dance attendance on anyone.
The new Director of the Royal Academy, *primer pintor*. Never contented.

Your *own work*! Monsters, witches, the diseased and the degenerate. Even in the sacred Cathedral of Valencia. For the boudoir of the Duchess of Osuna, witches sacrificing babies to a great horned ram! I saw your sketches. These aristocrats must have diseased minds. The Duchess, who has the finest dresses from England and France, the best kid shoes, and the most expensive hairdressers in Spain, pays you to produce demons for her boudoir!

You look surprised that your ignorant wife knows your work. Why should I not? I am the wife and sister of painters. But you do not know me.

A collection of prints and capricious subjects invented and etched by Don Francisco Goya. The author is persuaded that the censure of human errors and vices (although this seems the preserve of oratory and poetry) may also be a worthy object of paintings: as subjects appropriate to his work, he has selected from the multitude of stupidities and errors common to every civil society and from among the ordinary obfuscation and lies condoned by custom, ignorance and self-interest, those which he believes most appropriate to furnish material for ridicule, and at the same time fantasy.

Ridicule and fantasy. Those prints were on sale for two days in the shop right below us here, alongside bottles of perfume and liqueurs. Obscenities between men and women, all manner of other perversions. No doubt all this is true to life, but should it be made so public? *The censure of human errors and vice is worthy of an artist's attention.* Your own vices and errors included? Three hundred and twenty reales for a set. As much as an ounce of gold! So few purchased. Withdrawn after two days because of the Inquisition. You could not resist courting trouble. A good outcome, however – the pension you obtained for Javier by donating the plates and the unsold sets to the Royal Printworks.

San Antonio de la Florida. Fifty-two years of age, and here you are making frescoes for the Royal chapel, standing on scaffolding under the cupola, unable to hear the creak of an unstable plank, or a word of warning, with only young El Pescadoret to help you. Your reward – made Chief Court Painter and awarded five and a half thousand reales from their Majesties for a new carriage.

You walk among the ruins of Saragossa and find nothing glorious in war, only destruction and misery, rape and plunder. The heroism of ordinary people, too, but bloodied, nothing triumphant.

The works that have obsessed you for two years now, what you call *Los Desastres de la Guerra*. Your own work and magnificent. Magnificent because these etchings are so brutally honest about our war against the French since 1808. You find nothing glorious in slaughter, torture, rape. There are no victors. No pity. No purpose. *Nada* – the message from the grave.

Dark – cooler after the heat of the day. Clatter of carriages. People going to the Prado, to *tertulias*, assignations. Smells from the kitchen. I will not eat ever again. Where are you, Francisco? Come nearer, nearer; my time is short.

I need your forgiveness. Can you absolve me for the years of silence, for my coldness towards you? I have been most severely punished by God for rejecting you, for turning against Him. Almighty God, through the intercession of Santa Maria, has forgiven this sinner, and I have made my peace with Him. I am at one with the whole world, except you, Francisco. I hope that you will remember your Pepa fondly. Please say that you loved me a little, that Josefa Bayeu was as good a wife as she could be, despite the suffering, the deaths, the long absences, and the silences. Please give me a signal, Francisco, that you have understood me, that you forgive me? Just raise your hand and bless me.

I can no longer see you, husband. Come here to me. Whisper your forgiveness into my ear.

Thank you, thank you! Now I can go in peace. Please do not weep for me. I am ready to die. My only regret now is that my dear brother Manuel has not arrived in time. There is no more I can do for you. Our dear son will look after you. Gumersinda will care for you too ... or some other woman. You will not lack for affection. Call Javier and Gumersinda and dear little Mariano so that I can say goodbye to you all and go in peace to my Maker. Quickly!

7
THE DUCHESS OF ALBA
MADRID 1802

Journal extract
San Lúcar, March 1797

There he is, the arrogant fellow standing in front of me holding his palette like a shield, wielding his brush like a dagger. Totally ignoring my displeasure. Who on earth does he think he is?

'Excellencia, Maria del Pilar Teresa Cayetana de Silva y Alvarez de Toledo, 13th Duchess of Alba,' he is saying sarcastically, as if nothing has happened, 'why so churlish this morning? Please assume your pose. Let us proceed with the portrait. You can stop stamping your dainty silver shoe and take your hands off your wasp waist if you please. It looks so aggressive. Surely you do not want to have the whole world see this side of you? '

Oh, how he infuriates me! I want to wipe that mocking smile off his face.

'I am incensed Señor Goya because you are a treacherous snake. And an obtuse one. How can you think for one moment that I can pose for you who have spent the night disporting himself with one of my servants?'

Insolently he raises his penetrating black eyes and looks at me as at a child in a tantrum. Such a cool, detached, ironic, fearless look.

'My dear Duchess, I *am* surprised. You are jealous! And you call *me* treacherous. You, who have more dalliances than all the ladies of the Court together. You, who have taken so many lovers; actors, *toreros*, young students even. You, who have invited me here to this secluded place, although you are so newly widowed.'

I could strike his podgy face. I want to wrench away his palette and brushes. I have a mind to throw a jug of water over that portrait. But I do nothing. I sit there with my mouth open and my eyes blazing. Why do I not order him to leave San Lúcar at once? Can it be that I am afraid to cross this impudent commoner who has vastly overstepped the bounds of his social position? *Nobody* speaks to the Duchess of Alba as he has just done. Especially not such an old and ugly man, who is as deaf as a bedpost.

'Excellencia,' he says dryly, 'your face is twisted and sour. I shall paint you as a termagant if you so wish. Now, please readjust your mantilla. You should also tighten the sash. Good. Now place one hand on your waist and point the other to the ground.'

I obey but refuse to smile. He continues painting, a smug look on his face. I stand there like a sullen rebuked child and I ask myself once again how is it that I have allowed this man to become so familiar. To order me about like a servant. While I am standing in the pose he had commanded, I remember the first time I went to his studio in Madrid. I had heard of his liking for the bizarre, for the erotic. And I also knew that his work is admired by that old trout Maria Louisa, who fancies herself as an artist. So I had several motives for wishing to meet Don Francisco Goya. The portly creature, Maria Louisa, calls me *a bag of bones.* It was wonderful to hear how furious she was when I ordered a dozen copies of her latest French dresses and gave them to my servants to wear. Revenge is so sweet.

When I entered his studio he was standing at an easel with his back to the door.

He did not turn around. I remembered then that I had also heard that he had become deaf so I had to walk right up and stand in front of him and repeat myself. I told him to make up my face with the cosmetics I had brought with me. I did not fully understand why I wanted him to do that, to touch my face. It was not only because I had heard also that he was arrogant and I wanted to put him down, to show him my power. Commanding a great painter, so sought after, to be a lady's maid. If he was surprised by such a request, he did not show it. I have learned since then that it is not at all easy to read Don Francisco de Goya. He motioned me to repeat what I had said more slowly, then smiled in an annoyingly knowing way, as if he could also read the real reason. Without a word, he took the bag of cosmetics from me. He darkened my eyebrows like two black bridges, drew lines of kohl around my eyes, rubbed rouge into my cheeks, and dusted powder over my whole face until I sneezed. It was like he was playing with a doll. And all the time he held my face in his hands and a small smile turned up his full lips. He was humouring me, I realised, as a parent humours a silly child, or a lover cajoles a petulant woman. I, who had come to command him, had been reduced to childishness. It was then that I determined that I would have my revenge on him too, that I would enslave the insolent fellow. I would exercise the full strength of my charm and beauty on him. I realised that if I was to have power over this man, it could not be wielded simply because I am an aristocrat. However, I reassured myself that the task should not be too difficult. At that time I was still a beautiful woman of thirty-three, while he was low-born, at least fifty, rough-looking, and deaf. Not that it matters to me if a man is high or low born, as long as he is handsome and fascinates me.

After that first visit to his studio, I invited Señor Goya to Buenavista and commissioned him to paint a portrait of José and another of myself. For that portrait, I chose a deceptively simple white dress adorned with my favourite colour a wide red sash to show off my waist, a red bow on my breast, and another pinned on my hair. I even tied a red ribbon on the leg of my little dog at my feet. I know about colour too. The meaning of red.

But my plan of entrapment did not work as smoothly, or as quickly, as I had thought. Most men on whom I cast my eye succumbed very quickly and I do not believe it was only because of who I am. I know that when I pass by in the streets of Madrid people run to their windows to catch a glimpse of me. I am not blind. But this Goya fellow seems blind to my charms. He continues to treat me like a spoilt child. I am not a silly woman without a brain in my head. The most influential and enlightened men in Spain, including the poet Don Manuel Quintana, and the poet and philosopher Don Gaspar Melchor de Jovellanos are among my friends. The more indifferent he seems, the more determined I am to have him. In truth I am fascinated by this uncouth artist. I ask myself why this is so and have to admit that it is simply because he appears so impenetrable, contradictory and, most exasperating of all, unattainable. He has become my challenge.

In order to gain some foothold of understanding of the man, I have made it my business to get to know his work.

I visited the chapel which he had decorated for my friends María Josefa and her husband the Duke of Osuna in Valencia Cathedral. There I studied his mural of Saint Francis Borgia, one of her ancestors, who had given up his wealth and power as the grandson of King Ferdinand and become a Jesuit after his wife had died. I was startled by the sight of monsters and devils around the head of a dying penitent whom the saint is blessing. The painter had manifested the temptations and torments of us sinners in such a ghoulish manner.

At a private exhibition of his cabinet pictures for the members of the Royal Academy, I was struck by a picture entitled *Yard with Lunatics*, painted on pieces of tin with thick layers of brown paint depicting the inmates of the asylum struggling with each other while a guard raises a whip to flog them. The image of an isolated figure in the bottom right-hand corner, a woman sitting on the ground hugging her knees, has stayed with me.

Shortly after my husband's death I summoned him and commanded: 'I wish you to visit me at my estate at Sanlúcar de Barrameda.' I did not inform him that María Louisa had more or less banished me from Madrid. Jealousy is powerful in the hands of a queen. She wanted Manuel Godoy to herself. She could have him.

My invitation was a command. But I had to be careful that he did not understand it as such so I continued, 'I can promise you some interesting subjects for drawing and painting there.'

Now I realise that I had offered him precisely what I am so angry about this morning. I do not like admitting to myself that I cannot control everyone. Perhaps that is why I allow this exasperating man to order me about, why I cannot command him to leave San Lúcar. He would go, I am sure. And I would have lost my challenge. I am not used to this feeling of helplessness. I do not like it but we will go on. For now at least.

Sanlúcar is one of my favourite residences – I love it here, it is such a beautiful, quiet retreat. I feel I can relax and be myself, far from the intrigues and gossip of the Court and Madrid. Far from all the talk of our declaration of war on England and such follies. I want no news of politics. I have always felt that in this place I can indulge my imagination. And while he is here I can discover more about my intriguing resident artist.

Since his arrival he has spent the most part of every day drawing me, in all manner of poses. I, too, delight in opposites. One day I stand as demurely as I can in my most elegant clothes. Another day I nurse my little foundling, Maria de la Luz, on my lap. On yet another day I allow him to sketch me as I arrange my hair. He works so fast, in ink, chalk and wash, covering page after page of his album. The speed at which he works, the total absorption he displays are some of the things about him that intrigue me. I have never experienced absorption. I simply cannot seem to concentrate on any one thing for very long.

Sometimes I favour more erotic scenes. I tell myself that he is becoming excited, that at last I am beginning to hook my illusive fish.

But last night tells me that I was wrong. I have made the mistake of involving some of the servants. He made no objection. I made the further mistake of assuming that to him one body is like another, an object of form and movement. However, when I am tired of modelling he sends for the youngest and prettiest female servants. Especially one of them.

She is a pert young woman from Cadiz, with wide green eyes, breasts like pears, and the inappropriate name of Dolores.

The man is indefatigable. One would think that his age and recent serious illness would slow him down. And then there is the prodigious amount of hours he spends at his easel day after day, with little rest, even on Sundays. I have never met anyone like him, with his passionate belief in his own prowess, his phenomenal energy, his seeming disinterest in rank, his extraordinary fertile imagination and his fascination with opposites – the decorous and the obscene, the polite and the lewd, repression and complete freedom of expression.

My friends, and especially my maid Catalina in whom I confide many secrets, are astounded that I am so obsessed by this man. I am astounded myself. Not only are the discrepancies between us in birth, wealth, age and physical appearance so great, I feel I am his victim. I am furious with myself for having allowed such a thing to happen. Nonetheless, I must keep him near. I will have him. The struggle makes the prize more coveted. This is a new experience for me. Not a pleasant one, but I do not seem to be able to do anything about it. Is it because he is a great artist, I wonder? Because he possesses what wealth and birth cannot grant? Because he is beyond our reach? Is it because he sees everything differently that I want to get a glimpse of his world? I just do not know.

I thought until last night that I was getting somewhere. He has stayed on here long past the time to which he had originally committed himself. He told me that he had sent a message to his wife and young son waiting for him in Madrid, saying that his work is going very well and that he needs another month to finish it. I wonder how he will explain, if indeed he tells his wife such things, why it took him so long to complete one portrait. I doubt that he will show her those albums of sketches. I wonder what their relationship is. Does Doña Josefa ask to see her husband's work? Does she concern herself with his business? Does she wish to know where he goes? I somehow doubt it. For why should their marriage be any different from most? Matters of convenience. What husband discusses his business with his wife? And what wife shows the slightest interest in his life? We have our own affairs to occupy us. *Stand still! How can I paint if you twitch so, if you keep changing your expression?*

I will not, cannot, stand for this.

'You have dishonoured me in my own house,' I spit at him. 'How dare you treat me like a common *puta*?'

He does not look up from his easel. I have to go and stand in front of him and shout right into his face. His expression does not change. He looks at me coolly and I am suddenly afraid that he might pack his bags and leave Sanlúcar. And if that happens, what will he do with those albums of drawings of me in those poses? A man who dared to paint fallen women on the ceiling of a cathedral and then castigate the authorities because they objected would have no qualms about publishing those sketches.

And yet... what do I care if he publishes them? Let people think what they will. I live my own life. My grandfather brought me up to be free and to express myself however I choose. But one thing gives me pause. So soon after my husband's death. No, that would not be seemly. I would certainly have to object very strongly if Señor Goya is intent on selling sketches from that album.

As usual, he takes his time before he replies, as if deafness has granted him leave to keep me waiting.

'You do yourself a disservice, Excellencia. I doubt if a common *puta* would have your extensive repertoire of poses. Besides you enticed me here with promises, did you not? Why so exclusive all of a sudden? Why so vituperative? It spoils your expression. I fail to see why you are incensed.'

'Because, you old fool. I will not share you with servants, with anyone. I want...'

What have I just said? I could bite my tongue off.

He is studying my face intently. When he has read my blurted confession, he tilts his square jaw, juts out his lower lip and looks at me pityingly.

'You seem to forget that I have a wife and a son whom I love. You make a mistake in thinking that what you want you can always have.'

'A wife whom you love! You amaze me, Señor. Is this how you love your wife? Spending all these months here with me, making erotic pictures, far away from her and from your child? Taking advantage of my servant?'

He laughs, throwing back his great big lion's head. It is a strange sound, the sound of someone who cannot hear himself.

'I most certainly do not need lectures on how to love my family. As for taking advantage of Dolores, why don't you ask her why she came unbidden to my bedroom? Learn that not all men are your slaves, that wealth and position give you no god-given right to possess anyone. Learn also not to judge an artist by the same standards as you might other men.'

'How dare you be so familiar?' I shouted at him. 'And you, old man, you learn your place. You are a deaf nobody from some godforsaken village in Aragon. So remember where you are, and who you are, and to whom you are speaking.'

I am ashamed of myself as soon as I said that for I have never been one to look down on commoners or on anyone who has a disadvantage such as deafness. But of course I cannot admit this to him. He has already got the upper hand.

This time he does not keep me waiting for his reply.

'Let me tell you who *I* am, and to whom *you* are speaking. I am the greatest painter in Spain, the Director of Painting at the Royal Academy and the Court Painter. Moreover, I gained all these positions not because I was born a duke, not because I am handsome or can snare a Queen, not because I have inherited wealth, but because I have *genius*. As for my deafness, it is a blessing which protects me from hearing lies and stupidities. It enables me to listen to my own imagination. My deafness, in fact, gives me freedom to create my own inventions. And that is something *you* cannot do. You are a vain capricious woman with little to recommend her except a tiny waist and vast inherited wealth. You are intellectually and emotionally undisciplined. You spend your shallow life constantly seeking relief from your terminal boredom; you seek to consort with people like me in an attempt to share in our greater lives.'

I am dumbstruck by such rudeness. I splutter but cannot utter a word for I suddenly realise the truth of what he says. He knows me better than I know myself, than anyone has ever known me. I will never possess this man; no woman can, for he is possessed only by his genius. I realise that I will have to content myself, therefore, with what it pleases him to give me.

'Excellencia,' he says dryly, 'your face is still twisted. Is this the way you wish me to paint you?'

So I have to replace the mantilla I had thrown on the floor in front of him like a gauntlet and resume my commanded pose.

I have, however, insisted on choosing what to wear. I cannot bear to have my widow's black dress left drab and unrelieved, so I have chosen to brighten it with a red sash tasselled with gold and a deep yellow under-blouse with gold-encrusted cuffs. Red, yellow and gold suit me and provide a foil for my hair. I am also wearing my favourite silver shoes with gold toes and high heels. I have not removed my rings.

So far I have seen only the background for this portrait. He has placed me in the centre of a misty landscape in front of some trees. It looks as if I am on the sandy shore of a liquid gold river.

I am not allowed to look at my portrait until it is finished. When I am finally permitted to view it, what do I see? The insolent man has inscribed *Alba* on one ring and, incredibly, *Goya* on the other ring.

'What do you think you are doing?' I scream, 'I will not have your name on my ring. Remove it at once.'

Behind my display of rage, I am flattered. Is this not what I had plotted, that he would fall for me? My emotions are so confused by this man that I cannot think straight.

He responds by taking up his brush and writing the words *Solo Goya* in the sand, exactly where my finger is pointing.

'Now,' he says, 'that is the truth.'

'How dare you! I assure you Señor that I will never let anyone see this portrait. I will not be compromised.'

'Have no fear, my dear Duchess,' he replies coolly; 'you will not have to hide this picture because you do not own it. I intend to keep it for myself.'

'What? Keep it for yourself? The portrait I commissioned you to paint. You shall do no such thing. This is *my* portrait and *I* shall decide what is done with it.'

It is clear that this is not a battle of equals. That is what is really infuriating me.

'Really?' he says. 'I have not received one reale from you for this work. The painting is mine and *I* shall decide what is done with it.'

'But... but... I commissioned it. You have *refused* to take any payment. You said you would prefer to be paid when it was completed. I have been deceived. You *will* take my money and you *will* give me my portrait.'

'Does the painted object own the painting, or does its creator?' is his calm riposte.

'I am no painted object. I am the Duchess of Alba. This painting is of me. It is *mine. Give it to me at once.*'

But he just laughs his strange laugh and repeats, 'It is my work. *It is mine.*'

At that, he takes up his easel and walks calmly out of the room carrying my portrait, leaving me shaking with rage and frustration.

It is not my practice to keep such detailed journal entries but those months in Andalusia were a time of transition and mourning and I had recourse to my journal to express my confusion.

Shallow, capricious and wilful. Those words angered me at the time but I later dismissed them as the insolent remarks of a cantankerous old man who, because he considered himself a great artist, thought he could make such judgements of others. Perhaps I was capricious and wilful. I have lived life as fully as possible. But was I, am I, also as shallow as he claimed? As intellectually and emotionally undisciplined? Perhaps. In the past few months, since I began to feel ill and weak, I have found myself becoming more reflective, more unsure of what this life on earth means. Or perhaps what it should mean. What my own life has meant. For there is not much time left for me here, I believe. A shadow is coming over me.

After some months at Sanlúcar, Don Francisco returned to Madrid with his album of drawings. And with my Solo Goya portrait. I was more desolate than I ever imagined possible. In the days after his departure, I had time to think more deeply about José. In the early aftermath of widowhood, I have to confess, I had not allowed myself to give much thought to him or to our lives together. I had avoided grief. I had distracted myself selfishly with the vain pursuit of Don Francisco Goya.

I married José when I was thirteen and he six years older, and as the years passed and I gained some degree of maturity, I had come to admire and indeed to love him in my fashion. He was a kind man and he made no demands on me. We may not have had a great deal in common; he loved horse-riding and hunting, I participated in neither, he disliked dancing, I love to dance. He liked Haydn and I love *tiranes* and popular festivals, but we had no arguments. Sadly, our union was not blessed with children. In this respect, I have not been as lucky as María Josefa. How I have always envied her those four beautiful children. How tenderly Don Francisco shows her family in that unsentimental Osuna family portrait. There is no grand backdrop, no rich possessions on show, just contented parents with their children. The girls holding their fans, their brothers with their toys. Look at how affectionately he has painted little Manuela holding her papa's hand and Joaquina resting on her mother's knee.

I feel my childlessness sorely whenever I take a moment to feel sorry for myself and no doubt that is why I have surrounded myself with my waifs and strays. I love them all; besides my dear step-brother Carlos, they are the only family I have. I adopted my little pet Maria de la Luz so that I have someone to care for, to care for me. Surely everyone needs someone on whom to lavish affection and to be cherished.

A few weeks after Don Francisco Goya departed, my next guest Don Manuel José Quintana came to visit. Unlike Señor Goya, he sought to comfort me, composed poems to my beauty and my *scintillating intelligence.* But when I retired to the silence of my own apartments, I felt nothing but sadness. I dismissed Dolores and the other servants whom Goya had sketched, giving them handsome bribes to keep quiet about the activities on the estate. A few weeks later, I left Sanlúcar and returned to Madrid.

There I found Don Francisco busy with his Court work and, despite the economic recession, with many commissions from his other wealthy patrons. Although he complained that he wished people would leave him alone to live quietly and get on with the work he was obliged to do and to spend the rest of his time on what he called *things of my own*, he agreed to paint a group portrait of me with my family – Brother Basil, my lame old monk, my little Maria de la Luz, Luisito, Tomás's son, whom I also call my dear son, Pepita, and Trinidad, and Benito, whose mind is a little addled but no matter. Don Francisco came to Buenavista frequently. I found myself attempting to prolong the sittings. On some days I pretended I was too tired to pose. On others I claimed that one of my family was not available. So the painting proceeded slowly; the pace suited each of us for different reasons. That portrait was never finished. Don Francisco was overburdened with other commissions and I ran out of excuses to detain him. Neither of us insisted on its completion.

In any case, I had found other distractions. My passion to entrap the artist had cooled and I felt a sense of relief in going back to my former ways. Handsome young toreros are more exciting and much less troublesome than stubborn old men.

I did not lose interest in Don Francisco Goya the painter, however. I still wanted to experience his latest works. When I heard from María Josefa that he had produced half-a-dozen small paintings for their country house at Alameda, I had myself invited there in order to see them.

'They are pictures of witches,' the duke warned me, 'some of which you might find disturbing.'

I did not tell the duke that I am well acquainted with Don Francisco's strange subjects. But when I saw *The Witches' Sabbath* – a grotesque infant sacrificial rite to an enormous horned satanic goat – I was indeed disturbed. The image that most repelled me was that of a pole held by a bald half-naked witch from which the tiny grey bodies of naked infants hang like three dead rats. Goya clearly had become more obsessed with the bizarre.

Shortly after the witch paintings came the extraordinary *Los Caprichos*. I read in the *Madrid Daily* of the sixth of February 1799, in which *Los Caprichos* were advertised, a front-page article by him in which he stated that his purpose is to censure human error and vices because he believes these should be held up to ridicule. He went on to claim that his work is free from the influence of any other artist and from the demands of caricature. I simply do not believe either of the last two statements. I suspect that the wily monkey was simply protecting himself from prosecution on the one hand, and laying an inordinate stress on his originality on the other.

The Osunas told me that they had bought several sets of the eighty prints, which they invited me to see. My first reaction was astonishment; the audacity and obscenity in those prints simply stunned me. I had to examine them closer at my leisure, so I went to the shop where they were on sale, below Don Francisco's apartment in Calle de Desengaño. The Street of Disillusion – a most appropriate name for the home of such an artist. I disguised myself, wearing a thick beard and a tall hat and a heavy woollen coat. Just in case he was there, I did not wish to give him the satisfaction of seeing me buying his *Caprichos*. As casually as I could, I picked up a set of prints and asked the assistant the price.

'Three hundred and twenty reales, Señor. That is not expensive, if you consider that there are eighty prints, which makes it only four reales for each one,' he replied with what I thought was a suspicious look at my beard.

I growled: 'Are there many sets available?'

'Yes, there are plenty of them remaining. However, since grandees like the Duke of Osuna have purchased four sets already, I am sure that other grandees will very soon follow suit.'

'In that case I'd better buy a set now before they are all taken.'

As I was walking towards my carriage, I looked back and saw a woman and a child emerging from the house. I stopped for a moment to watch them. The woman was short and plump. She wore a simple bonnet; her face was lined with worry, and her clothes, though well-made and expensive, were not at all fashionable. She had the hermetic air of someone who speaks little. I was conscious of a sort of envelope of silence surrounding the woman, as if she, and not her husband, were deaf. She was holding her small son's hand and looking down on him as if he were the Christ child. I had never witnessed such a look of adoration. I lowered my head to hide the envy in my heart and hurried into my carriage.

In the privacy of my boudoir I spread out the prints in a circle on the floor and walked around them. I stared at them intently one by one. I was once again overwhelmed by his vision of the world: such a pessimistic, eccentric and cynical judgement. There is no redemption in those works. Corruption, hypocrisy, cruelty and mendacity reign. Here is a surgical dissection of Spanish society: the Court, the Church, marriage, the law, doctors, the arts and sciences, the healthy and the diseased, the able-bodied and the deformed, rural life as well as the streets of Madrid, poetry and philosophical ideas – nothing appears to have escaped his inspection and condemnation. As if to show his originality as the creator of such an amazing body of work, Goya has placed a self-portrait as the frontispiece, depicting himself as a man of importance, solid in his success.

Three of the prints in particular struck me. The first one, the *author,* as Goya styled himself, is entitled: *They say yes and give their hand to the first comer.* It shows a slim young woman, whom I recognised immediately, the green-eyed creature from Cadiz, being led blindfold by ghoulish, grinning men. A hideous mask is tied to the back of her head, and the sinister figure of a man standing behind her is also wearing a mask. A wizened old woman, the matchmaker Celestina, raises her hands in warning, resignation or despair. Grotesque heads loom in the background and another Celestina, waving a stick, is leading a frenzied mob. So Goya is saying that women go into marriage blindfolded, but so, he seems to contend, do men. The marriage contract is doomed to fail. The ghouls give such a warning. Does he live unhappily in a failed marriage? Was his wife Doña Josefa led blindfolded towards him? Am I wrong in assuming that his prints are autobiographical?

Another of the prints which arrested my attention is a parody of a hunting scene in which three females, two young women and one crone, set up a trap to catch unwary lovers, who, once caught, are plucked and put on a spit. *All will fall* is Goya's caption and his own face is caricatured among the trapped figures. Could this mean that he had fallen into my trap after all? I had to sit down for a while to consider that. Two young women. His own face among the trapped figures. We are all victims. Is that what he means? *All will fall.* In love, into folly, into disillusion?

Dreams of falsehood and inconsistency – that is what he has titled the print which most upset me. It is a direct comment on me, showing his poor opinion of my character. *How he must despise or even hate me,* I thought when I first examined it. But could that mean that he also might love, might have loved me? Is not hate the other side of the coin of love? I was thrown into considerable turmoil for days.

When I considered the entire set of eighty prints I concluded first of all that his theme is the exposing of deceit. All the prints depict people pretending to be what they are not, people playing cruel tricks on each other. Such a parade of degeneracy, of criminality, of superstition, of cruelty! Prostitutes, hanged men, deformed and degenerate people, victims of the Inquisition, witches, ghouls, abused and dead babies. I remembered the other dead babies hanging like rats on the pole in the *Witches' Sabbath* and wondered if these savage images arose from Goya's anger at and grief for the deaths of his six infants, about whom he spoke one evening after dinner at Sanlúcar when he was drunk. On further reflection, I think it more likely that the *Caprichos* are political satires and caricatures of high society. The print which convinced me that this is indeed the case is the one with the legend: *Neither more nor less*, in which a monkey, holding a paint brush and a palette, sits in front of an easel and paints a donkey that is sitting up on its hind legs and wearing a judge's wig. So that is how Goya regards his sitters. And how he sees himself – as the clever tricking monkey!

More recently again, I have reflected on the layers of meanings in those prints. They are, I think, both caricatures and social and political commentaries. Don Francisco reflects the terror and chaos that engulfed us at that time. Spain was sliding towards disaster. Criminal gangs roamed the country; nobody could walk safely in the streets of Madrid after dark. His friend, Don Gaspar Melchor de Jovellanos, the former Minister for Justice, the voice of enlightenment, was in exile in Gijon, ousted from the government by Godoy who was Prime Minister then. The exchequer was impoverished. The dreadful events in France, the King executed like a common criminal after his own citizens voted for his death sentence in what they call the National Convention, sent waves of terror through all us grandees in Spain. The political situation here was dangerously unpredictable. Catastrophe was in the air. All-pervading grievous discontent hung over the country like the plague.

The Osunas invited me to Alameda shortly after I had bought and studied *Los Caprichos*. I was intrigued to find that my hosts and their guests had devised elaborate charades, based on the prints, in which the King and María Luisa and her current lover Manuel Godoy, were played out as figures from the caricatures. I observed that the Osunas did not include themselves as subjects in these charades. We all deceive ourselves, in minor or in major ways. How right Goya is.

The Duke and María Josefa have been good and generous patrons of Don Francisco Goya for many years. Count Floridablanca introduced him to them. She told me that the Count had extolled the talents of a Señor Goya, saying that he deserved all the patronage he could get, for he was a most fascinating and unusual character as well as being an extremely gifted artist who could talk about anything – Italy, the theatre, theories about art. And when he told her that Señor Goya was also an expert on the corrida, I expect that really convinced her that she had to meet the painter.

She is more of an aficionada than I am and has often been seen at the corrida with her protégé. He makes a grand entrance in his wide-brimmed hat, close-fitting jacket and full cloak. He also carries a sword.

'We have wonderful discussions about the merits of our favourite toreros. Don Francisco considers that Costillares is the best and that Pepe Hillo comes a close second. We disagree on that issue as I am certain that Pedro Romero is the finest torero,' she told me excitedly. That is not surprising as Senor Romero is one of her protégés. She is not the only one who favours toreros.

'When Pepe Hillo was killed after having fought a thousand corridas, Don Francisco was inconsolable for weeks,' she continued with a shake of her head and a look of remembered sadness.

I was sorry too but in my view Hillo was lucky to have survived having been gored a dozen times before he met his end.

'Don Francisco adores hunting. He often rides out with the Infante at Arenas de San Pedro and also hunts with my husband. As you know, I also love riding.'

So they have quite a lot in common. I wonder what else they shared.

María Josefa has a great many talents and gifts. So elegant, so learned, so accomplished. She manages her own estates and is president of the women's section of the Economic Society of Madrid. She is also a devoted mother, taking care of all her children, not abandoning them totally to nurses and servants. If I were a jealous woman I could really resent her. But I do not. I admire my friend. I may have many faults but jealousy is not one of them. In any case, she is a decade older than me. I believe Don Francisco Goya was her portrait painter with whom she shared a passion for the corrida and horse riding, nothing more than that.

Until now, I never had much in common with him. Except vanity, I suppose. I was vain about my figure, my lustrous hair and my youthful beauty. And that man is still as vain as any woman, with his fine jackets imported from France and his expensive boots and hats.

Don Francisco must have produced over two dozen major works for the Osunas. I have seen most of them in their various residences over the years. And what a variety of contrary scenes. Rural idylls, happy children playing in the sun, juxtaposed with scenes of highway robbery and murder. Such eccentric, unpredictable and unflinching expositions of the evil as well as the good in the world. In my opinion he is a more subtle Hieronymus Bosch. He does not avoid suffering, evil or cruelty. He flatters nobody.

He does not flatter María Josefa either. He has painted her long face as it is, her thin nose, her rather protruding eyes. He depicts her truthfully as she is; an intelligent, elegant woman of style, if no great beauty, in her dark blue silk robe à *l'anglaise* with her matching pink bows, her hip pads decorated with roses and her ringletted hair arranged under a straw hat, just as I have seen in the Cabinet des Modes. I am sure that had he portrayed her as a raving beauty, she would not have commissioned any more work from him. María Josefa is not vain and she is certainly no fool.

The hermitage of San Antonio de la Florida is situated on the banks of the river Manzanares on the outskirts of Madrid. The land around the hermitage belongs to the King and Queen, to Godoy, and to me. We developed an exclusive residential quarter there and also built a small neoclassical church, which has become a centre for fashionable worship. The King required frescoes for the apse and the cupola. Jovellanos, who was back in power, with my assistance, secured from the King the lucrative commission for his old friend Don Francisco de Goya. Thus, I was able to view his daily progress after he had gone home for the night, and even on some occasions during the day when his young Valencian assistant was painting in the church alone. Knowing Don Francisco's need for artistic freedom, I convinced the King that he should be allowed free rein and that no restrictive iconographic demands should be made of him.

I am well acquainted with the art of Tiepolo and other great Italian masters, so I was surprised by Don Francisco's approach to the frescoes in San Antonio. His heavy, separate brushstrokes, his fierce stippling and dabbing and streaking seem to me to be unique; as is the portrayal of seductive females and predatory males among a largely brutish multitude which crowds the dome of the church. I recognised some *Caprichos* characters, which both slightly shocked and much amused me. The man is most certainly original. I decided to speak to Manuel Godoy that night. Through him, I could arrange almost anything. And so it was that soon afterwards Goya was promoted to Principal

Court Painter. He will never know that he owes that position to me. Not that he does not deserve it on his own merits. But then merit does not always bring its just rewards.

Godoy reminds me of Goya and I now understand the basis of some of my former fascination with the Prince of Peace (the infatuated María Luisa bestowed this title on him after his victory over the Portuguese troops in the silly War of the Oranges). Like Goya, Godoy has risen from an obscure background, although his origins in the minor aristocracy are of a higher status than Goya's. It is well known that as a handsome young officer of the guard, he caught the eye of María Luisa, who took him into her bed, made him a duke, a member of the Privy Council, head of the Royal Academy of San Fernando, and finally Prime Minister. It is also common knowledge that she also bestowed on him one of the crown properties, an annual salary of a million reales, a beautiful young wife – the daughter of the Infante Don Luis – and a large part of the Infante's fortune and art collection. Such is the price of such outrageous lust. She has made a laughing stock of the royal family. She is completely without shame. How does the King endure her? What will her children think of her when they are older and realise what their mother is? Especially the youngest one, the little Infante. Will he discover who his father is?

Whatever Godoy wants happens. And what Godoy wants, he has often impressed upon me, is a modern, enlightened Spain. What Godoy also wants is for the arts to flourish. Godoy, therefore, is good for Goya. And that is all fine and well for as long as Godoy remains in favour and can exercise his power. And his remaining in favour is far from certain. He may have the protection of the Queen but his reforms have made him very unpopular and he is widely disliked. So Godoy may not always be good for Goya.

I heard from Godoy that Goya was engaged in making equestrian paintings of the Royal Family and that he made the same artistic demands on them as he did on all his sitters. María Luisa was exhausted by his demands. She had to spend hours at a time mounted on a plinth set up in the King's apartment, wearing her heavy riding clothes.

'It is torture. That man Goya is a slave driver for his art,' she told Godoy, who gleefully retold the story to me.

'I pity the poor horse that has to suffer her bulk,' I said. 'She is jealous of my style, my elegance, my figure, my friendships, my conquests, and indeed of all my activities. Queen or no, she is still a lump of lard, a dull creature.'

'Her Majesty is quite a good artist and an excellent horsewoman. A narrow waist, beauty and a sharp wit are not everything in a woman,' Godoy replied, with the look of a neutered well-fed lapdog.

Despite the torture she endured while Goya painted her, the lump of lard was apparently very pleased with the finished work, and especially with the portrayal of Marcial, a present from Godoy and thus her favourite horse. Her Majesty was also delighted with the progress of another big painting on which Goya was engaged – a group portrait of the entire Royal Family. Godoy told me that she admired just as much the sketches of each member of the family because they show how Goya has laid his colours on the prepared canvas. The King, however, was less pleased as he complained to Godoy that he had to pay out a fortune for painting materials. Good old Francisco, he spared nobody. Poor blind María Luisa was convinced that when the royal group portrait was finished it would be the most magnificent in all Europe. I was sure it would be technically excellent and I was also certain that it would not show her in any good light. He would not flatter even the Queen.

Godoy confirmed my suspicion. He told me that he had seen the painting in its final stages and that it is an enormous canvas depicting thirteen members of the family. It makes nothing of their royal rank, although they are dressed in impressive sashes and most elegant clothes, there is no sign of monarchy, no throne, no royal insignia.

'How has he depicted María Luisa?' I asked.

'As she is.'

Well, that is fat and ugly. I did not say this to Godoy. I wanted more information from him.

'And how is her hair painted?'

'I did notice that she has a cupid's dart in it.'

A cupid's dart! How comic. On an old woman like her.

'What about her dress? '

'Very elegant. In fact, quite like the one you are wearing now.'

She always copies me. I was delighted to hear that she had copied me again, as that style was sure to make her look as plump as a turkey. I took delight in imaging how unattractive she must look and how blind she must be not to notice Goya's making a spectacle of her.

'Tell me more about this magnificent painting.'

Godoy looked sharply at me. 'You have such a sharp tongue and you are so rivalrous with Her Majesty that I don't think it is a good idea to tell you anymore. '

'Oh, don't be silly,' I laughed. 'Go on, you know you love a good gossip as much as the rest of us.'

'Do not tell anyone then that I have discussed the painting with you. It is not yet finished and I am sure their Majesties would not like it to be discussed before they are ready to have it unveiled. '

'I promise not to say a word.'

'Well, Goya has included himself in the picture, standing behind Doña María Josefa.'

'Ah. Like Velasques in *Las Meninas*. '

'Something like that, I suppose.'

'And the little Infante, how is he treated? '

He looked annoyed that I had singled out the child. 'Why do you ask?'

'No reason. Just that Don Francisco loves to paint children,' I said.

I suspect that the child resembles his father who everyone is sure is not the King.

I did not meet Don Francisco Goya for some years after our abandoned family portrait. He was too busy working on his royal commissions and besides he may have wished to avoid me. I had no desire to see him as I had recovered from my obsession. Obsessions rarely last long with me. I had many other affairs, distractions and amusements to fill my days. So I was surprised one day a few months ago when I received a message from him requesting to see me.

To tell the truth, and the truth is something I am trying more and more to face, I was amazed by my reaction; I found myself as excited as a young girl in the bliss of first love, as giddy as the Queen always maintains that I am. I plotted that meeting like a campaign. I had my maids lay out all my dresses, my sashes, jewellery, my shoes. Finally, I chose my white dress with the gold border – to remind him of his first portrait of me. I caught myself in the mirror and laughed a bit shamefacedly at my silly behaviour. But I still cancelled all my appointments and invited him to visit me the following day.

He arrived in a grand carriage, wearing the most fashionable clothes, clearly designed to let me know that he was to be treated as a *hidalgo*. I had heard that he now wished to be addressed as Don Francisco de Goya. I greeted him with as much sangfroid as I could manage, while aware that my cheeks were treacherously glowing. His attitude was cool and business-like. As if nothing had happened between us. That was surprisingly hurtful. I kept my voice cool and my manner as distant as his. He did not waste time telling me why he had sought to see me.

'Don Manuel Godoy has asked me to create some special works for him – to do with sexual freedom and the sensuous attractions of women, I thought at once of you,' – my heart leapt – 'as a model,' he continued.

I knew then that I had not recovered. The man had only to stand in front of me for me to be entrapped once more. *Foolish woman*, I told myself. *He clearly cares not a whit for you or the time he spent with you in Sanlúcar.*

This time I made him wait for a reply. Truthfully, I was sorely conflicted. If I refused to act as his model for what sounded like a risqué project: special works for Godoy to do with *sexual freedom and the sensual attractions of women*, I might never see Don Francisco de Goya privately again. And if I agreed...?

'Did Manuel ask for me to be the model?'

'No, he did not. He left that up to me.'

'I am flattered that you thought of me. There are many younger women you might have considered.'

He looked at me with something like interest then.

'There are indeed lots of pretty young women but what is needed is a woman of experience and that you certainly are.'

Was he aware, I wondered, of my relationship with Manuel Godoy? Had he been following my amorous adventures since he last saw me?

'What kind of paintings do you have in mind?'

'What I shall paint are two contrasting works, both full-length, the first of a *maja* wearing exotic oriental clothes lying on a couch, and the second, of the same woman – naked.'

Naked! He intended to paint a woman, a real woman, not a goddess or mythical figure naked. What a scandal that would cause! Something in me loves scandal. But I had to put up some defence. Some pretence.

'You astound me, Señor. You think – do you? – that the Duchess of Alba will expose herself thus? You imagine that I would allow myself to be the object of entertainment for Godoy and his leering friends.'

He just raised one eyebrow and smiled. 'I could, of course, find a real *maja*, but I remembered how fond you are of erotic poses, what an exponent you are of sexual freedoms. I imagined that you might welcome another opportunity to indulge yourself.'

I almost choked. He had not become one whit less impudent. I was about to snap that I had no intention of being used in such a manner, when the thought of not having him near again stopped me. I was on the point of saying I would agree to his request, on one condition: that he might paint my body but must replace my face with some inconsequential woman's features – but he did not wait for me.

'Of course, you realise I would have to use another woman's face. Though your body, as far as I can see, has not lost its attractions, you are thirty-eight now, Excellencia, and your face is too old, I am afraid, to be that of a credible *maja*.'

I thought I would have a seizure. I was to be a headless body, displayed flagrantly for the delectation of Manuel Godoy and whomever of his lecherous friends he wished to entertain. What stopped me from summoning the servants to show Señor Goya the door? Possibly the same reason that I had not thrown him out of Sanlúcar. Who fully understands their motives? Besides, motives are not fixed, they ebb and flow like the tide.

'May I choose the clothes and the pose?' I heard this little girl's voice asking. Santa Maria, what had become of me?

'You may choose the clothes, as long as they are oriental in style and I approve of the colours. As for the pose, I will tell you which positions to adopt.'

Because I was amazed to discover that I felt newly shy in front of him, I asked him to paint the clothed *maja* first, but he said that *he* would decide which he would start with. He had not changed.

When the work was about to begin, he told me that he would paint the two pictures more or less at the same time, but that he would begin with the naked painting. He set up two easels and prepared two canvases.

'Lie with your hands behind your head,' he directed when I had undressed and was lying on the couch. 'Now, raise your right elbow behind your ear and clasp your hands behind your head. Good! Now turn your right hip towards me and look at me. No, not straight at me. Look at the side of my face.'

The same brusque commands as in Sanlúcar. The model as puppet.

I obeyed without a murmur. 'Are you not going to prepare my face?' I asked almost timidly. Dios mio, I could have kicked myself. Abasing myself like that.

'There's no need. I told you I will use another's face.'

I realised that I wanted his touch on my skin. Is there an end to foolishness? As the work progressed, with me lying naked on a satin-covered couch, looking not quite straight at the man who evidently and most irritatingly still possessed my mind as no man ever had, I had to struggle to maintain my composure. That same feeling of frustration and lack of control which had so infuriated me in San Lúcar returned. I was relieved that my face was not going to be painted and I did not therefore have to suppress the visual expression of my feelings.

After a week working on the naked painting, Goya instructed me to dress for the next day's session. I selected my favourite colours and dressed in a saffron yellow gold and black embroidered waistcoat, and a salmon-coloured sash which I wore over diaphanous Turkish trousers. I also chose gold oriental slippers and enormous ivory satin cushions; all of which, luckily, met with his approval.

As the work went on day after day in silence, I became aware of a change in Don Francisco. Nothing that I could voice. Something softer, considerate even. For from then on, before he started work on the canvas each day, with great gentleness, he made up my face, blackening my eyebrows and outlining my eyes with kohl, rubbing rouge on my cheeks, reddening my lips and powdering my face as he had done on that first day in his studio. I was absurdly grateful for this attention.

I was to assume the same pose as before, placing my arms behind my head and leaning against the pillows in an attitude of availability.

'Raise your knees slightly,' he said as he tucked the white filmy trousers suggestively between my thighs. He tightened the sash under my breasts so that they were pushed up further into roundness. Then he told me to look sideways at him and to keep a small secret smile playing about my lips. I lay there looking at him, tense with excitement, throbbing with desire. He seemed very pleased with the effect I had created.

'Godoy will love this. Just the degree of suggestiveness he likes,' he remarked.

I squirmed and once again was grateful that my face would not be shown. Who would know the identity of the model? I have no distinguishing mark on my body, no moles or such and there are other women with as small a waist.

And so the paintings progressed, Don Francisco working for a week at a time on one canvas, and for the next week on the other. Fearing that my contentment would last only as long as the painting continued, I attempted to delay progress. I pretended I had a headache or that I had to leave Madrid on urgent business. I did not know then that that I would have no need for pretence of illness, that my fake headaches would soon become only too searingly real.

The painting of the clothed and the naked *maja* continued spasmodically for more than two years. Don Francisco did not seem to be in any hurry to finish. That was greatly surprising. I remembered how fast he had worked in Sanlúcar. Now he worked slowly as if he, too, wished to prolong the time we spent together. He worked, as usual, in silence. When the session finished for the day we still did not speak much and never about Sanlúcar. I found it pleasantly refreshing to be in the presence of a mainly silent man. I asked him once about *Los Caprichos* and told him I had purchased a set. 'Good,' he said and went on painting, muttering that he had to concentrate on what he was doing.

'I am not painting an idealised mythical Venus. These paintings are of a real woman, real women. This is a first in the history of art, you realise. Your body will be famous.'

Nobody will know it is my body. That will remain a mystery for art historians to attempt to solve. I took delight in imagining their conjectures.

'And your face is immortalised already by the poets. And in the first portrait I painted of you.'

We did not discuss the Solo Goya portrait which had so enraged me. I trusted that he had kept it for himself as I had not heard from anyone who might have seen it. Had Doña Josefa seen it, or his son Javier? I somehow doubted that.

Often weeks or months passed without a sitting. Some days he seemed distracted, lines of worry rippling his forehead. *He looks exhausted. What can I do to help him?*

'You know, my dear Duchess' he suddenly broke in on my thoughts, 'you are not looking at all well.'

'What do you mean? I assure you I am quite well. It is *you* who looks ill.'

'I mean that you are paler than usual and your eyes are dull. You are much too thin for a woman of your age. Do you have another of your headaches?'

How did he know I had been having the most dreadful headaches? I never mentioned them. As he spoke, I had the most dreadful headache, a raw pounding behind my eyes, which had gone on for days. I had not slept for three nights and had not been able to eat properly for weeks. I did not tell him, or anyone else, however, as he was sure to have insisted that I see a doctor. I have always preferred not to know what might be wrong in my body.

The ferocity of my headaches has not lessened, nor has my appetite returned. I have become thinner and thinner, until I really am a bag of bones. Don Francisco made no further mention of my condition and painted me as I had been in my prime in Sanlúcar. So he is capable of flattery, after all. Kindness might be a more apt word. I had to muster all my strength simply to lie on the couch without moving my aching limbs. Perspiration soaked my body and face. Fever was a slow burning furnace in my breast.

'We will stop now, my dear. We have done enough and you are fatigued,' he said, putting down his brush and, taking a handkerchief from his pocket, came over to me and dabbed the perspiration from my forehead and my upper lip. I caught his hand and thanked him silently. I had to look away, unable to bear the pity in his eyes.

I collapsed one day not long after that as I was undressing for the painting. He rushed towards me, lifted me onto the couch, dressed me and called one of the servants to fetch a doctor at once. When I regained consciousness I tried to persuade everyone that the hot weather had overcome me momentarily. I tried to struggle to my feet, but fainted once more against the pillows.

The doctors are still puzzled by my illness. I sometimes think doctors simply guess at the cause of illness, that they are often as mystified as we are. Unless one has a broken bone or something painfully obvious, they treat us in the dark. My doctors argue among themselves as to possible causes for my headaches, loss of appetite, the deathly pallor of my face, the dark circles under my eyes. And not one of them has come up with a cure or even some treatment to alleviate my suffering. I spend my days on a couch. I refuse to confine myself to a dark bedroom, away from my family. They flock around me, the dear ones. They give me such comfort.

There have been no more painting sessions, but to my delight and surprise, Don Francisco continues to visit me.

'Please do not fret,' he has reassured me. 'I can finish the work from my sketches. I have enough done now. You have not let me down.'

He regales me with hilarious tales of the gossip at Court and in the city. The truculent man has become a witty and considerate entertainer. I am astounded and gratified by the change in him. I would not have considered him capable of such softness, of such thoughtful kindnesses. One does not, cannot, know other people. We judge them too quickly or too harshly and fix them in those judgements as if no change were possible. I have come to realise that none of us is simply understood, that all of us have depths and qualities, as well as failings and vices which we do not recognise because of our own fixed opinions, false certainties and erroneous perceptions.

'I want you to design my tomb,' I told him one day last month.

He is the only one to whom I can speak about my death, which I am certain cannot be far off. The body does not lie. I feel the chill of death in my bones, in my blood. He is the only one who does not pretend that I will recover my health, who does not try to convince me that my doctors are curing me; the only one who does not appear to be afraid of death.

I find extraordinary comfort in the company of the man whom I could not conquer when I was in my prime, when all Spain was at my feet, who now, when I am wasting away, when my once luxuriant black hair has dulled and thinned, when I am as skeletal as a plague victim, has transformed to become my most loyal and loving friend. He is willing to come to me whenever I request him. He deserts his work for María Luisa and the King to be with me. I remember him telling me in Sanlúcar how he had given up his work when his beloved Javier was ill as a child and I flatter myself that he cares deeply for me too.

He has brought me a sketch of his design for my tomb. He showed it to me with tears in his eyes. 'Wonderful,' I said, 'exactly as I had conceived it.'

Yesterday we sat together peacefully in the garden so that I could get some fresh air and escape the sick room for a little while.

'Is it not amusing,' I said, 'that we, who could not agree on a single thing, are now of the same mind concerning my tomb?'

He replied by taking my hand, as scrawny as a crow's foot, raised it to his lips and kissed it.

'My dear Francisco, it is almost worth dying to see you thus,' I said and I laughed. 'Will you promise me one thing?'

He moved his eyes slowly from my lips to my eyes and back again. 'The *Solo Goya* painting – will you keep that yourself? You will not sell it?'

I have changed my mind about that painting. I am no longer angry that he wrote his name on my ring and on the ground at my feet. I now believe these signatures to have been a sign of his love for me, no matter how he tried to disguise and deny it at the time. So the painting should remain our secret.

'I promise. How could I part with it? And when I die, I will leave it to my son.'

I knew I could trust him. I will sleep calmly tonight. Before he left this evening I had one more question for him

'Francisco, whose face will you use for the *majas*?'

'I have not yet decided. Perhaps Godoy will want his latest mistress, Pepita Tudó.'

'Could I make a suggestion? If it is possible, would you paint the face of Dolores? You remember Dolores, don't you? She came to Madrid some years ago, after that time in Sanlúcar and recently she has come here to live with me. She loved posing as you may remember and she was a good model, was she not?'

Bygones are bygones.

'Your wish is my command,' he said with a sweeping bow.

'That's one of my wishes, of my dying wishes.'

I could not prevent myself from breaking down when I said those words. I am only forty and I have so many things I wished to do before I die. I have lived a frivolous life, I know. I have often been capricious and wilful. I have amused myself in foolish ways. Yet, I have lived life to the full. I hope I have not harmed anyone and have helped a few. I intend to do some good before I die. I have already looked after my dear family very well in my will. 'Your dear son, Javier, shall have ten reales a day for his lifetime.'

His eyes filled with tears. 'That is most gracious and generous of you,' he said. He understood it for what it is, a token of my affection for him.

'I shall leave Madrid very soon, while I am still able to travel. I shall go to Andalusia. It is peaceful there and I am deathly tired. Tell me this Francisco; you are an old man and you have been seriously ill, yet you have such energy, you are indestructible, from where do you get such energy, such passion?'

'You aristocrats are not a healthy lot,' he replied with a wry smile, 'although the weak among you sometimes survive; while we are tough, because only the fittest among us live beyond infancy. As for passion and energy, one is born with such gifts. And one develops them, burnishing them against the rough corners of this world. Passion is the child of struggle. Energy is the engine of passion. But do not include yourself among the degenerate aristocrats, my dear Cayetana. For you are more beautiful, kinder and more generous than any of them.'

You are more beautiful, kinder and more generous than any of them. The author of *Los Caprichos.* The man who flatters nobody. I cannot see for tears.

8

DOLORES
MADRID, 1802

Here is how I came to live with the Duchess of Alba; how I know our greatest artist, Don Francisco Goya, and all that has happened to me since the my life changed in the Spring of 1797 in Sanlúcar Barrameda.

Her Excellency had promised us servants a holiday so that we could have our picnic. I was very excited because I had only recently started to work at the Duchess's residence at Sanlúcar Barradmeda and I had heard that picnics were often the beginning of romances among the servants. I was fourteen years old and had never had a romance. Not because I did not desire it, but because my older sister, Pilar, watched over me like the strictest mother.

I was walking across the courtyard to the servants' quarters thinking about what I would wear the next day and how I would make myself noticed by Manuel, one of the grooms, who had a kind, honest face and a humorous smile, when a gentleman stepped down from the Duchess's carriage, and instead of going up the steps to the house, looked over in my direction, and started walking towards me. He was a shortish, square man, wearing a tall hat and a long woollen coat which was far too heavy for Andalusia. *He must be either ill or crazy,* I said to myself.

'Good afternoon, Señor,' I said, because I could not avoid speaking, as he was almost upon me and had not spoken.

He did not reply and I just said to myself: *Dolores, why do you imagine that the Duchess's guests would recognise us common people? You should wait until you are spoken to, and not presume to greet one of them. Pilar says that we are like so many ants to the grandees. We have no names, and our function is to work ceaselessly for them. Although ... they do say that her Excellency, grandee as she is, acts like an ordinary human being sometimes. She can joke and laugh like one of us. Of course, at other times, they say, she is as high and mighty as the Queen herself.* I often gave myself a good talking to. Maybe it was because I had no mother and only an older sister to scold me.

Anyway, this man who did not speak was standing right in front of me, staring at me as if I was an unusual butterfly that he might like for his collection. Now, I had often had to deal with such behaviour from fellows in my village, as well from some of the Duchess's men. Santa Maria, I do not mean *her* men! I mean her male servants – the gardeners and stable boys. This behaviour I am talking about, it is like this: coming up and standing in front of you and staring, as if they had never seen a woman before. Or waiting until you have passed by, and then pinching your behind. The cleverer ones tried to engage you in talk; they flattered you, saying all sorts of stupid soft things that no girl should believe, although I have to admit at times I was tempted to believe some of them. Still, I managed to keep myself pure and clean. *Dolores*, I told myself, *when the right man comes, you will know. And so you had better keep yourself pure for your wedding night, or you might miss your chance of a good husband and a comfortable life.*

Where was I? Oh yes, the short man with the black hat who stared at me as if he was measuring me for something, or else trying to engrave my face on his memory. *Maybe I remind him of his daughter*, I said to myself and waited for him to finish his examination. I was standing there in the middle of the courtyard, it seemed for ages, and the man was still saying nothing, just looking, so I finally asked respectfully in a low voice, 'Are you looking for your quarters, Señor?' And when he did not attempt to answer me, I thought, *well, this one is very arrogant indeed.* Then he put his hand to his ear and signed that he was deaf, and I was ashamed of myself for thinking him arrogant. I smiled and repeated what I had said, moving my lips really slowly and hoping that he might read them.

At last he spoke in a strange accent I had never heard before.

'What is your name, girl?'

'Dolores,' I said smartly, 'but I never feel sad or sorrowful.'

I don't know why I said that. It was forward of me. Maybe I just wanted him to know that I understood the meaning of my name. I also wanted to let him know that I did not like being stared at, even if he was old and deaf.

When I said the bit about never being sad or sorrowful, he sighed and said: 'Fortunate girl, you are luckier than me.'

As he spoke, his whole face was like a plate of pain and his shoulders sagged. I felt quite sorry for him. I was staring at him, I suppose, by then. He seemed unwell to me, sort of hazy or milky around the eyes, and his mouth looked as if he would love to cry, but could not, being a man and all that. We stood there in the courtyard, two strangers in the place, just looking at each other mutely.

'What age are you, Dolores?' was his next question.

'Fifteen,' I lied, 'I was fifteen in January.'

I had to lie because I had told the housekeeper who hired me that I was fifteen, and that I had already had some experience as a maid.

'What an exquisite little *maja* you would make,' he remarked.

Then he raised his hat and smiled at me, and went off with the servant who had come to take him to his quarters.

Having no idea what a *maja* was, I asked Teresa when we were folding sheets in the laundry room that evening. She was one of the Duchess's maids who had come with her from Madrid.

'A *maja* is a poor woman from our class who goes to Madrid and makes a life for herself there. *Majas* wear mantillas and fancy clothes and carry poniards in their garters to protect themselves and, let us say, they live a free life. They live among *majos*, who are supposed to protect them. These *majos* are great dandies who wear tight knee-breeches, buckled shoes and embroidered jackets. They conceal a knife called a *navaja* in their sashes, and are given to parading the streets in long capes and puffing black cigars. Some of them play guitars and tambourines and are popular with noble ladies; just as *majas* are with wealthy men. You would not want to tangle with those people, Dolores, they're all very tough.'

Fancy clothes, tambourines, a free life; it sounded most attractive to me, I must say.

What a wonderful picnic we had. I wore my white dress and tied a scarlet sash of Pilar's around my waist and pinned a red rose in my hair. Manuel noticed me right away and behaved in a very friendly manner towards me. He was most considerate, helping me over the rough ground, and making sure I was not sitting on any thistles, and that I had the choicest pieces of meat to eat. I got to thinking that perhaps he could be the right one. Still, when he tried to kiss me behind the stables on the way home from the picnic, I held back, because I was not sure if he was the right one, or if I only thought he was the one because there was nobody else. There could be a Ramon or a Joachim or a Carlos waiting around the corner, who would be just as handsome, and perhaps with better prospects. One of those might be the right one for me. How was I to know?

On the day after the picnic, Her Excellency sent for me and I ran to her apartments right away. Shaking I was, wondering what I had done wrong to bring myself to her attention. I had been working at Sanlúcar for less than fifteen days at the time and had never spoken to my mistress. I had seen her only from a distance, but had heard a lot of things about her. They said she was the most powerful woman in Spain, apart from the Queen, but that she was much more beautiful, charming, and elegant than the Queen. Teresa said that she had heard that the Queen was jealous of our Duchess, but that she could not ignore her because the Duchess of Alba was on such intimate terms with the most powerful men. *Caramba!* When I heard that, about being on intimate terms with the most powerful men, I did wonder what exactly was the nature of these intimate terms. That's what I was like then, Pilar used to say, too nosey for my own good. *Curiosity will get you nowhere*, she said, *only into trouble*. But I did not believe her. Because if you do not wonder about things, if you are not curious, you don't learn new things; you don't know about people who are different from you. And, really, everyone is different from you, so you can always be curious. Like I was about the Duchess of Alba.

I was so surprised when I went into her room. Close up, she was completely different to what I imagined such a wealthy and powerful woman would look like. She was like a bird, so slight, with the smallest bones and a tiny waist. She had this fountain of black hair, even thicker, curlier and longer than mine. Her face was round, which was a surprise, because she was so thin everywhere else. She had eyes like a thrush – quick they were, intelligent and darting. Her nose was long, like mine, but not as pointed. *That's the one thing that's wrong with your looks, Dolores,* Pilar always said, *your nose is too long and too sharp. It makes you look older and more experienced than you are.*

'Are you Dolores?' the Duchess asked, raising her head from a book.

'Yes, Excellencia,' I said, doing a sort of bow, which I thought was necessary when speaking to a Duchess.

'I believe you have already met Don Francisco Goya,' my mistress went on, her sharp eyes taking me in with great interest.

'I don't know that I have,' I said.

'He is the man you met in the courtyard a few days ago, just as he arrived.'

'Oh yes, Excellencia, I remember now. He was wearing such heavy clothes and we had a strange accent.'

'Don Francisco is an artist, and he has come to Sanlúcar to paint and to draw. Have you ever seen the work of an artist, Dolores?'

'Well, I have seen the paintings on the wall in the cathedral in Cadiz, Excellencia.'

'Don Francisco is such an artist, but artists do not only create frescoes for churches. They also paint portraits of people and other sorts of pictures – pictures for private patrons. Don Francisco is a very important man. He is the Court Painter, which means that he is one of the most important artists in Spain. He paints pictures of the King and the Queen and many of the grandees at Court.'

I thought she would never stop talking about this famous Don Francisco Goya. I stood in the Duchess's grand room, listening to her posh Madrid accent, and wondering why she was telling me so much about this man, unless she was going to assign me to be his particular servant or something.

'How old are you, girl?' she asked suddenly.

'Fifteen,' I lied again. I was beginning to find lying quite easy.

'You look older than your age,' she said, and she looked as if she was thinking about something.

Must be my sharp nose, making me look more experienced, like Pilar says. I shifted about on my feet a bit, wondering when she was going to tell me to look after this famous artist, but she lay there on her chaise longue, occasionally looking me up and down as if she was making up her mind about something.

'Don Francisco would like to use you as a model for some of his pictures,' she said at last. 'You will be required to pose for him for a few hours every day.'

'Me, a model!' I said, startled. 'But, Excellencia, I do not know what it means to pose. I am a good laundry maid and chambermaid, but I know nothing about pictures, or poses, or artists. I would not know what to do, Excellencia.'

I was forward, wasn't I, talking to the Duchess like that? But I was afraid that I would be found wanting. She laughed, a really strong laugh from such a slight body.

'You silly girl,' she said, 'you do not have to *know* anything. All you have to do is to follow whatever instructions Don Francisco gives you. You will be sent for whenever he is ready to draw or paint you. Of course, you will be relieved of your normal duties while you are working for Don Francisco. And if you are a good model, you will receive twenty reales extra at the end of your service here.'

Twenty reales extra! That was a fortune to me. *It will be the start of my dowry. I should be able to get someone a bit better than a groom with such a dowry.* And I was curious. What would this 'posing' be? What instructions would I be asked to follow? If I had had any idea of what was to come, I should have left her Excellency's employ that very day. That is, if I had been a good girl like my sister expected me to be. But I was a very different kind of girl to Pilar. Even if I had had it all spelled out for me, in every detail, I believe I would still have done it for the reward of twenty reales. And also out of curiosity.

'Now there are some instructions I have to give you before you start this work for Don Francisco. First of all, you are to come promptly when he sends for you. Artists are temperamental people, and must not be kept waiting when they are ready to start work.'

She saw my face then. 'What *is it*, Dolores?' she asked with a little irritation.

'Please, Excellencia,' I stammered, 'I do not know what "temperamental" means. Does it mean artists have a bad temper?'

She laughed her strong laugh again. 'Not exactly, but it does mean that their moods can change quite quickly, so that they could become annoyed easily if their wishes are not met at once.'

'Oh,' I said. 'Like the cooks.'

'Yes, like the cooks. Now, you must do whatever Don Francisco asks you to do – without objection. Artists have their own reasons for what they do and must not be questioned. It destroys their concentration and they need a lot of concentration to make a picture. Do you understand?'

'Ask no questions,' I said smartly.

'Good. Thirdly, artists work in a very private way. They cannot have their pictures discussed until they are finished and ready to be displayed in the church or wherever they have been painted for. So you must not discuss what goes on during the time you will be modelling for Don Francisco. Not with the other servants, or your family, or with anyone else. Do you understand that clearly?'

'No discussion with anyone,' I said. These instructions were easy.

'What family have you, girl?' the Duchess asked.

'Only my sister, Pilar, in Cadiz. My father died two years ago, and my mother died when the last baby was born. My mother had eight babies. Pilar and I are the only ones who lived.'

I was rambling on about my family because I was so nervous, and I always talk too much when I feel nervous.

'I see,' she said, quite slowly, as if she was really thinking about what I was saying and was sympathising with me in some way. I did not know what her *I see* meant. Had she had a lot of dead babies too, or did her parents die young like mine? Anyway, it was nice to have the sympathy of a Duchess.

'So,' she said suddenly in a firm voice: 'I have given you three rules to remember before you start to work as a model for Don Francisco. What are they?'

'Always come immediately, ask no questions, and don't discuss the pictures with anyone.'

'You are a clever girl, and will do well,' the Duchess said, with another smile: 'There is one more thing I have to tell you. Don Francisco will also paint and draw portraits of me. If you happen to see any of these, you are to follow the same no discussion rule. Is that clear? And finally, he may sometimes require several people to model for him at the same time. The same rules apply in that case as well – no questions, and no talking about what goes on with anyone. Now have you understood everything I have been saying, Dolores?'

I nodded and repeated her rules.

When I went back to my work, I pondered on what the Duchess has told me. I could hardly wait to find out what being a model for an artist meant. I also wondered why there had to be so much secrecy about it. I was soon to find out.

Three days later, Don Francisco sent for me. I was to go at once to the Duchess's apartments, where a servant would show me into the studio where he was working. I went just as I was, in my servant's dress, because I remembered the first rule – *go the moment you are sent for.*

Don Francisco was standing with his back to the window when I came into the room. He looked much less burdened without his heavy coat, and he also looked a good deal healthier than on the first day I had seen him. He was wearing a white shirt, open at the neck and a long, loose, black gown, trimmed with turquoise blue satin and tied at the waist with a sash of the same colour.

'Ah, Dolores, the little *maja*,' he said, smiling. 'Are you ready to be an artist's model?'

'Yes, Don Francisco,' I said, slowly so that he could read my lips. 'I am ready, but I don't know what a model does.'

'Just follow my instructions and you will learn quickly,' he said in his strange deaf man's voice. 'Here are the clothes I want you to wear today.'

Lovely clothes they were. Finer than anything I had ever touched; a yellow dress with a sort of a V drop at the waist, a trim of gold at the hem, and long tight sleeves embroidered with gold thread. *It must be the Duchess's*, I thought; *such a beautiful dress.* It was a little too short for me, but it fitted me everywhere else, as if it was made for me. I had to wear silver shoes with high heels and a black mantilla covering my hair. I went behind a screen and put on these wonderful things, and when I came out Don Francisco looked at me approvingly, and then arranged my hair so that it fell over one shoulder. The first day all I did was to stand without moving for hours while Don Francisco drew in his album.

'Do not look at me,' he ordered. 'Look to one side, as if you were thinking of something sad that has happened in your life. Has anything sad happened to you, even though you have told me you are not sorrowful like your name?'

'Well, I was very sad when my father died two years ago. I don't remember my mother very well. She always seemed to be ill. Or having babies.'

'Oh, so you have many brothers and sisters?' he asked, showing a deal of interest.

'No, Señor, I have only one sister. Pilar.'

'And the others? What happened to the other babies?'

'All dead, Señor.'

'And your poor mother. When did she die?'

'A long time ago, Señor, when I was four. After our last baby sister died.'

'How many babies died?' he asked, as if he really wanted to know the answer.

'Six altogether. Four before Pilar and I were born, and two afterwards.'

Don Francisco looked really sad when he heard that. I said to myself, remembering the Duchess's sympathy as well: *These grandees are human too.* I was not sure if he was indeed a grandee, but the Duchess had spoken of him as if he were. In any case, it was pleasant to receive sympathy from such quarters, and I felt as if I was somehow a special person because I was an orphan, with only one sister left out of a family of eight.

Every day for the next week he sent for me. The other servants began to get jealous. 'What's so special about you?' Teresa asked. 'You're supposed to be a laundry maid, yet you haven't washed a sheet for days and you spend all the time in the Duchess's apartments. What do you do there all day long?'

Just as the Duchess had instructed me, I did not tell her what I was up to. Don Francisco made scores of drawings of me. Sometimes he asked me to lean on a table, or to look over my shoulder as if I was expecting to see someone. I got pins and needles standing there, but I did not mind because I felt so special to have been singled out from all the servants. I certainly did not miss having my arms immersed in hot water, and my hands rubbed red raw with washing. I loved wearing the fine clothes and the elegant shoes. I loved, too, the silence in the room while he was working at his drawings. Sometimes he used a pencil, and sometimes he used ink and a brush. But he always worked fast, not saying a word.

After another week, Don Francisco told me that he wanted me to do different poses.

'You are a good model,' he said,' and you have learnt quickly. Now, do you think you are ready for some more daring positions?'

'I am, Don Francisco,' I answered, not having an idea what he meant by *daring positions*, but curious and anxious to please, and pleased also to be told that I was a good model and a quick learner. I was soon to learn about daring positions.

'I want you to take off your undergarments,' he said.

Take off my undergarments! I was shocked but then I reminded myself of what Her Excellency had told me about artists and I did what I was told. Don Francisco waited until I had slowly taken them all off. My face was burning, but he did not seem to notice.

'And now, turn your back to me and look over your shoulder directly at me... Good... Now lift your skirts with both hands... No, not like that! Lift them up, girl... higher!'

I lifted my skirts to above my knees. 'Is this up far enough?'

He replied by coming over from his easel, taking my skirts and pushing them up to my waist at the back.

'Now hold them there.'

I was horrified. I was to hold my skirts up so high as to expose my backside, and I had no underwear on! *What on earth would Pilar say if she saw me now?*

'Try not to look like a startled child,' Don Francisco growled. 'And look directly at me as if you enjoy what you are doing.'

Well, *that* was a difficult instruction to follow, so I thought of how much I had enjoyed the picnic, and how I had felt when Manuel said I looked beautiful in my white dress with Pilar's crimson sash and the rose in my hair.

'That's better,' Don Francisco said. 'Now we are getting somewhere.'

After that day, the poses Don Francisco asked me to do became more and more curious. I was to look angry and frustrated and pretend to tear my hair. I was to clutch my head as if I had just heard that my sister had been murdered. Some days the Duchess was in the studio, too, just watching me, and also watching Don Francisco. I found that difficult. It was hard enough to do those strange things when there was nobody else there, but I felt very self-conscious when she was looking at me. But after a while I got used to her presence and paid no attention to her. I just acted the parts I was to play as best I could and Don Francisco said he was delighted with me and that I might be ready for what he called *more advanced poses. Well,* I wondered, *what could they be?* But I was not frightened. I wanted to continue to be a quick learner and to be rewarded with my twenty reales.

'Have you ever pleasured yourself?' Don Francisco asked me one day when I had been posing for him for about two weeks.

'Do you mean do I have fun dancing and the like?'

'No,' he said, 'not dancing.'

Well, I could not imagine what he was talking about. 'Eating sweetmeats or chocolate?' I asked.

He laughed heartily at that and I was glad the Duchess was not in the room to witness what a stupid girl I was.

'Come here and I will show you what I mean,' he said gently.

I went over to the table where he kept his albums of drawings and he placed three pictures in front of me. I cannot tell you how shocked I was. I gasped. Not that Don Francisco could have heard me, but he saw my face. *Santa Maria*, I did not know where to look.

No questions, the Duchess had said, and no discussion of what went on in the studio. *Santisima Virgin Maria. What would Pilar do if she could see what I've just seen?* And then I wondered if Pilar had ever pleasured herself. Or if any of my fellow servants did it.

'My goodness, you look blooming these days,' Manuel said one morning as I was crossing the hall on my way to pose in the Duchess's apartments. 'You seem different. Not so childish – more experienced – or something.'

I just smiled at him. Then he asked me if he could take me to the fiesta in Cadiz. I said it depended on whether or not the Duchess wanted me that day, and off I went, with my head in the air, and my mind filled with how beautiful I was becoming. And desirable.

The Duchess was already in the studio when I arrived.

'We have something new for you today, Dolores,' she announced when I had taken off my work clothes and draped them over the screen. 'Don Francisco tells me that you are learning how to be a very good model indeed. As I told you, he also paints and draws me, and today I have decided that he will draw us both together.'

I was horrified when I heard that. Surely the Duchess of Alba did not intend to permit a mere servant to see her naked! The Duchess laughed when she saw my expression.

'Dolores,' she said, 'you must not be shocked. Things are permissible for art's sake which would not be proper in normal circumstances. You have to realise that the human body is a beautiful object for the painter's brush. He sees it as a shape, like a lovely tree or a flower, not as a person. Unless, of course, he is painting a portrait, and even then he sees the face as made up of different shapes. The artist does not think to himself: *I am painting a nose or a mouth*; he sees shapes and shadows, and that is what he paints.'

The Duchess knows a great deal about art, I said to myself. *And such an intelligent woman must be correct.* So, when she told me to lie down on the couch beside her, I did so without much bother. I just kept saying to myself: The *Duchess knows about art. What would an ignorant girl of fourteen like me know?*

And when, in the afternoon, they brought in another girl, whom I recognised as one of the Duchess's personal maids, and asked both of us to lie with the Duchess while Don Francisco drew us, I felt quite relaxed. In fact, I said to myself: *Dolores, you are growing up very quickly. These are the things that adults do.*

Don Francisco made us do a lot of different poses together. Like me and the other girl sitting naked back to back. And other really daring ones. I have to confess that while all this was happening, I felt really excited. My nipples became as hard as little pebbles, and I was wet between my legs. I felt my whole body flushed and pulsing. He sat at his easel and drew picture after picture of us. He seemed removed from us, like he was outside a window, and not part of what was happening in front of his eyes. His eyes flew from our bodies to his easel and back again. Sometimes he came forward to get a better view, and at other times he stood back to look at his work. The drapes were drawn and the room was quite dark except for the candles which flickered all around us. *It is like an altar in the church*, I thought. It was also extremely hot and airless and after an hour I was exhausted just from lying on a couch!

'That is enough for today,' Don Francisco announced.

I was really glad to hear him say that. I jumped up and ran to put on my clothes. The other girl, whose name was Carmen, I found out later, did the same, but I noticed that the Duchess stayed where she was, naked on the blue velvet couch, her long hair tumbling over the ivory cushions.

'Remember girls,' she said as we left the room. 'You must not speak to anyone about our work here.'

She looked quite strict when she said that, like one of the nuns at our convent school. That struck me as really funny afterwards, a naked nun on a blue velvet couch!

Carmen and I looked at each other, and I knew that she felt as embarrassed as I did and that neither of us would dare tell anyone what had gone on in that room

I had been modelling for about three weeks when Don Francisco sent for me one evening. That was unusual because he normally wanted me during the mornings and sometimes during the siesta hours. I knew the rules well and asked no questions, but I have to confess that I was surprised to see two other men in the studio when I walked in. I recognised them. One was a gardener and they were both friends of Manuel. They were wearing clothes, I was relieved to see. The Duchess was not present and Don Francisco was talking to these men, giving them instructions about where they were to position themselves. I wondered if I was to watch them doing something and I grew excited at the thought. But he told me to take off my clothes and to go and sit on a chair, which he had placed in the middle of the room.

I froze. No man had ever seen me naked. Don Francisco did not count because he was an artist, and he did not see the human body as a person, only as shapes and shadows. I could not undress in front of Manuel's friends. I kept seeing Pilar's outraged face, hearing her saying: *Do not disgrace our family, Dolores. How could you hold your head up in the village if any of this were to become known? These men will boast that they have seen you naked. They will surely tell Manuel. Your honour will be sullied and you will never find a decent husband. Tell Don Francisco that you do not think this is art. Tell him that you have compromised your honour enough already.*

Don Francisco was busy setting up his easel and getting his materials ready. When he turned and saw me unable to move, a look of desperation on my face, his face softened, and he said more gently than I had ever heard him speak: 'Is this too much for you, girl?'

I nodded bleakly, wringing the edges of my apron.

'Is it because you have never been naked in front of a man?'

I nodded again. 'Except yourself, Señor. And the Duchess says that artists are not like other men.'

With that, the Duchess suddenly appeared from behind a screen, came over to me and took my arm quite roughly. She had obviously hidden in order to watch what was supposed to happen, and she was angry that she had had to reveal herself.

'Now, come on, you little prude,' she whispered, her face thrust right into mine and her eyes as cold as ice. 'You agreed to model and to ask no questions, and now you are causing difficulties. If this continues, I regret that I may not be able to pay you the twenty reales I promised you.'

The twenty reales! *You have already done a lot of things you did not dream of before*, I said to myself. *And now you are going to risk losing all that money; as well as annoying Her Excellency and Don Francisco. She will send you back to the laundry room, where you will have to slave in hot steam, destroying your hands and breaking your back. Besides all that, you will lose your chance to get a dowry and a good husband. Whatever you choose to do now will affect you for the rest of your life.*

Don Francisco, the Duchess and the two grooms watched me struggle with my conscience.

'All right,' I said, at last. 'I will do what you want; as long as you make these men swear that they will never speak of what happens in this room.'

My humiliation had made me bold. 'And,' I continued breathlessly, 'I want *thirty* reales.'

The Duchess snorted, but Don Francisco said in a commanding voice. 'It shall be as the girl requests.'

The Duchess turned to the men, who were both looking at their shoes. 'Swear that you will never disclose what happens here today.'

They nodded like dumb idiots.

'Speak up,' hissed the Duchess. 'Let us hear you give your word of honour. And remember you will not be paid a peso if you as much as utter a single syllable. On top of that, you will never work again if I hear a whisper from anyone about Don Francisco's work. Is that understood?'

The men then swore by the Virgin that they would never say a word, even to their wives.

'Now,' Her Excellency said, turning to me with a grim face, 'you have delayed enough, Dolores. Get undressed at once and do exactly as Don Francisco tells you.'

She went behind the screen again and I had to undress right there in front of those men. Don Francisco seemed to feel sorry for me and said quietly: 'Now, Dolores, please go over and sit on that chair.'

It was the first time he had called me by my name for weeks. *He really is a kind man,* I said to myself. *I will be safe with him.*

'No, I don't want you to sit like that, with your legs together. You must sit as if you were on a horse's back. Good, that's it!'

Then he called the two men over and made them sit on the floor right in front of me. He took his drawing board to the side, where he could see all three of us. I still blush when I think about what he had me do next. I closed my eyes and when I opened them the two men were grinning like fools and licking their lips. Don Francisco was busy sketching and again seemed as if he was outside everything, on the other side of a window. The Duchess came out from behind the screen then, her bodice all undone and her skirts tucked up. She seemed to be almost as excited as the two men.

That night I could not sleep. I lay awake planning what I would do with my thirty reales. I decided that I could do better than a mere groom like Manuel for a husband. The realisation that I could not stay at Sanlúcar dawned on me. No matter what the men had sworn, I could not face them day after day, wondering if they had told anyone, and seeing the look in their eyes.

By morning I had decided that I would make my way to Madrid, with the help of Don Francisco. I was sure to find a wealthy husband there. I would send for Pilar as soon as I married, install her in my house and find her a rich husband too. I may have been only fourteen years old, but I felt like an old woman of twenty-four.

Don Francisco seemed to have decided that I had been tested enough for the present and during the next week he gave me easy poses to do. He gave me a red and black flounced dress to wear and fixed a black lace mantilla on my hair. 'Now you are my little *maja*,' he said, and he drew me standing, sitting or lying on the couch, but always fully dressed and demure. God forgive me, I became quite bored after a few days and I missed the excitement of the advanced poses.

The Duchess came to the studio during those days, but she did not stay long, as she had done earlier. One day she did not appear at all and I decided that I had better make my move.

Don Francisco's bedroom was next to the studio. (I knew that because one morning when I had arrived a few minutes early, I had seen him emerging from it wearing his nightclothes.) We finished quite late that day and he seemed fatigued. He went straight to his bedroom while I was still behind the screen changing out of my costume. I waited until I heard the bedsprings creak, and then I quickly took off my clothes, crept into the room and slipped into his bed beside him. Of course, he had not heard me coming and did not realise that I was there beside him until I put one hand on his shoulder, and with the other felt under his nightshirt for his member. The candles were still lit, and the room was quite bright. Without turning towards me, he murmured a name I did not catch.

I pulled his face towards mine, so he would know who was in his bed. He looked old and cross, but he smiled when he saw it was me.

'My dear little *maja*,' he said, 'this is not part of your work, you know.'

'I know that, Don Francisco. But I am not a child any more, and now I want to become a woman.'

'In that case, it is probably better to become a woman with an old man who will not harm you, than to give yourself to a young fellow who might destroy your good name with his boasting.'

He made love to me very gently. He held me when I cried out in pain.

'From now on, you will feel only pleasure,' he said.

'But why did you take out your member so quickly?' I was bold enough to ask him.

'Because, Dolores, you do not want to have a baby. You cannot afford the disgrace and, besides, a baby would severely hamper your ambitions, would it not?'

How could he have read my mind? I told him then about my plan to go to Madrid with my thirty reales, find a wealthy husband there and send for Pilar. I told him I would suffocate if I had to stay in my small village and end up marrying a poor labourer. I could not bear to have many babies who would not survive, and then die young myself like my mother had.

'Oh, my dear girl, I can see that Her Excellency and I have changed your life. We have played God. I only hope that you will not suffer.'

'But you must help me!' I cried. 'You are the most famous artist in Spain and you know all the important people, even the King and Queen. You can introduce me to high society, can't you? You can help me to find a rich husband. Please.'

But he shook his head and took my face in his hands.

'My dear little ambitious Dolores,' he said 'you must not expect this of me. I have a wife and a son and others for whom I am responsible. I am afraid that you will have to make your own way in Madrid.'

I started to weep, but he took little notice.

'The Duchess will pay you handsomely for your work. I did not seduce you. You came freely to my bed. Perhaps I would have been wiser to have rejected you, but I did not want to hurt your feelings. With your spirit, I am sure you will make your way in the world quite easily.'

I wept more when I heard this and knew that he would not help me. I told myself that I had been a foolish girl. I had given away my virginity for nothing. And I wept again because I knew also that my life would never be like Pilar's; that I would have to look out for myself in a strange place from now on. But after some time I allowed him to comfort me and let him wipe away my tears. I was like a disappointed child. I *was* a disappointed child – a sinful child who had taken part in her own corruption and was angry because she had not got all the earthly rewards she had expected for the sins she had committed on her immortal soul. I am glad to say about him that Don Francisco did not take advantage of me. We fell asleep and were not aware that the Duchess had come in and had seen us.

That was the last time I saw Don Francisco. I was not asked to model again and had to go back to my work in the laundry. He left the estate a few days later. I saw him get into the Duchess's carriage, carrying a great album of drawings. *Who will see those shameful pictures?* I wondered. For that is how I had come to regard them. I no longer believed the Duchess's grand speeches about art and artists and the beauty of the naked human form. *Dolores*, I berated myself, *you have allowed yourself to be used to amuse wealthy people. You have allowed your girlhood to be cut short, and now you are unable to content yourself to become the wife of peasant or a carpenter. You are such a foolish girl that you have lost your virginity to an old man who has now left Sanlúcar with lewd pictures of you. If Pilar finds out what you have done, she will never speak to you again.*

As for those men who had seen me in the studio, I had to go to great lengths to avoid meeting them. Once I came across them sniggering behind the stables when I was carrying my heavy basket of sheets to the clotheslines. I hated them. I hated the Duchess. I hated Don Francisco. And I loathed myself.

'What has happened to my pretty Dolores?' Manuel asked. 'Why so surly and discontented?'

'It's none of your business,' I snarled and ran away from his hurt and puzzled face.

At the end of April the household was in a fever of packing and closing up rooms. The Duchess was departing to Madrid. She sent for me before she left. I went into her apartments and found her just as bad-tempered and out-of-sorts as me.

'Here are your thirty reales. If Don Francisco had not insisted that you be paid, I would not be giving them to you.'

'But you promised,' I stuttered.

'That was before you seduced Don Francisco,' she said and her eyes were like burning coals. 'You are a little trollop. You dared to abuse my goodwill.'

'But... But...'

'But nothing. You are dismissed from my service. Never show your face in Sanlúcar again. Now take your money and leave.'

She threw open the door and practically pushed me out.

That is all the thanks you get for obeying all her shameful orders and for being a source of excitement for her. She calls me a trollop. So there is one rule for her and quite another for girls like

*me. It is so unfair. Pilar is right, we are like insects to people like
her. We do not merit respect.*

'What's the matter with you?' Teresa asked when I swept
into our room.

'Shut up you, you simpleton,' I hissed.

She sprang back as if I was a viper.

I packed my few clothes, hid my fortune in my
underclothes and left Sanlúcar that very day, determined to
go to Madrid, where, if all else failed, I would become a *maja*
and live a free life, and carry a poniard in my garters.

That is the whole story of how my life was changed that
distant spring. I came to seek my fortune here in Madrid and
I have had many adventures since then. I managed to find
myself a rich lover by whom I have had two sons. I named
the first-born Francisco and the second Manuel. Because my
lover was already married, I could not send for Pilar as I had
promised myself and I had to continue lying to her about
my life. Perhaps she suspected something, but she made no
mention of any suspicion in her letters. All she asked was: *Why
do you never come back to Cadiz?* I wrote that my housekeeping
duties left me no time for travelling so far.

I set about becoming a lady. I learned to read and write,
I learned to play the clavichord, I found a French tutor. I had
my dresses copied from the French styles. And I kept up-to-
date about the work of Don Francisco Goya. When I read
in the newspaper that he had produced a set of prints which
were on sale, I asked my lover for three hundred and twenty
reales. He complained that it was a lot of money but I told

him it was for something special for my birthday and he gave me the money, as he always did in the end. I took a carriage to Calle del Desengano, where the advertisement said the prints were on sale in a perfumer's shop. As I was about to go into the shop to make my purchase, there was a great flurry at the doorway and servants in very splendid uniforms opened the door for some grandee, a lady dressed in the most splendid dress I had ever seen, finer even than those I had seen the Duchess of Alba wear.

'Who was that?' I asked the perfumer when the lady and her entourage had departed.

'That was her Excellency, the Duchess of Osuna,' he replied proudly. 'She bought four sets of Don Francisco de Goya's *Los Caprichos* prints. Now, what kind of perfume would you like, Señorita?'

'As a matter of fact, Don Francisco de Goya is an old friend of mine,' I said haughtily, 'and I too wish to purchase a set of those prints.'

The look of surprise on his fat face!

Back in my room, I examined the prints for images of me, or of the Duchess of Alba, for I was sure that Don Francisco would have put to use some of the many sketches he had made of us at Sanlúcar. I recognised myself in the print which he had entitled: *They say yes and give their hands to the first comer. How true*, I thought. *How true. I was blinded by my own greed for the Duchess's thirty reales.* He used my face or my figure in other pictures, too, but that did not bother me. In fact, I felt quite flattered. These prints are so strange and fantastic, so pessimistic, that I could not understand them at first, but I examined them every day, and thought about them, and finally I began to understand something about Don Francisco which I could not put into words at that time.

'A message for you,' my maid told me one day when I returned from a fitting at the seamstress's. 'A man came here this afternoon saying he had been sent by the Duchess of Alba to give you this letter. He said that he will return for your reply tomorrow morning.'

She was most impressed that the Duchess of Alba had sent me a personal letter. I acted the grand lady and swept the envelope out of her hand. As I opened it, I puzzled how the Duchess had discovered that I was in Madrid, and how she had found out where I lived.

Dolores, she wrote, in a rather unsteady hand, *I have been feeling rather ill recently and ... I would like to make some amends to you for what happened at Sanlúcar. I wish you to come and live with me. You would have no work to do and will be treated as my daughter. Please consider my proposal and let me have your response as soon as you can.*

The Duchess of Alba requesting me to consider her proposal, almost *begging* me to go and live in her palace! I took my time replying. I had not seen her for almost six years; she could wait for a few days.

'But I do not understand,' my lover said. 'How does the Duchess of Alba know you? Why does she want you to live with her?'

'When I was fourteen years old, I worked for Her Excellency at her estate in Sanlúcar, near my home village.' I said. That answered his first question and I had no intention of answering the second one.

And that is how I came with my sons to live here at Palacio de Buenvista with the Duchess of Alba.

What a shock I received when I was shown into her apartments. She was unrecognisable, both in looks and manner. Gone were the rosy cheeks, the perfect skin, the deep sheen on her hair. She looked ill and pale and even thinner than before. Her sparkling eyes had dulled to embers. But, as I was to discover over the next days and weeks, what was most surprising was the change in her character. Although she had always been gentle with her foster children, like Maria de la Luz, now she spoke so softly and kindly to everyone, and was not in the least petulant or arrogant. I was treated like a daughter, as she had promised. The Duchess was most contrite about what had happened at Sanlúcar and determined to do everything in her power to recompense me for what she called *the theft of your girlhood*. I told her that in fact I did not feel cheated. I had learned so much that spring, that Sanlúcar had started my transformation from an ignorant illiterate country girl to an educated woman.

'My ambition now is to marry a wealthy man who can take care of me and who will accept my sons. I know that will not be easily achieved, but I can be very persuasive and persistent. I may have to pretend initially that the father of my boys has died.' I told the Duchess who looked doubtful that such an ambition was realisable.

'Oh Dolores,' she sighed, 'wealth does not bring happiness and finding such a man as you seek will not be easy.'

Pilar! To my shame I had not written to her since I came to live in Buenavista with the Duchess. What would I tell her? How could I explain why the famous Duchess of Alba had invited me to live with her as her daughter? I imagined her married to a decent artisan in Cadiz, with several children – perhaps one of them named after her long-lost sister. When I had succeeded in my ambition, I would go to Cadiz, find Pilar and her family, and bring them to live with me in my grand house, if they wished to come. I would give them whatever they needed.

Don Francisco came often. I did not see him, but the Duchess told me that he had painted two large paintings of her, one of her naked and one of her as a *maja*, dressed in a Turkish costume. I was surprised that she had been willing to be painted naked because these pictures would probably be widely viewed. She saw my look of surprise and explained that she would not be identified because the face portrayed would not be hers.

'I'm a little too old to be a believable *maja*,' she said with a wistful sigh. 'We will have to find somebody young and beautiful.'

'Would you allow Don Francisco to use your face?' she asked some days later. I was flattered. Somebody *young and beautiful*. I would be famous! My face painted by the Court Painter! I was about to agree, but then I said that I would like to meet him before I gave my answer.

He looked old and worn-out and his elegant clothes could not disguise a somewhat battered look about him.

'Who are these paintings for?' I asked, no longer feeling inferior or afraid. 'I wish to know before I decide.'

'They are for a very important man.'

'I'm sure they are. A painting of a naked duchess by the Court Painter must be for an important man, and a rich one.'

Don Francisco laughed when he lip-read that.

'Dolores,' he exclaimed, 'how you have changed! How confident you have become!'

'It's many years since Sanlúcar. I was a naive peasant girl then. If you tell me who these paintings are for, I may agree to allow my face to be used.'

I really have grown in confidence! Indeed, I can be quite brazen. I no longer need to obey instructions. The Duchess has settled a sum of money on me, which is sufficient for me and my children to live on modestly for a few years at least. Regret and guilt make for good sources of income.

'The paintings are for Don Manuel Godoy,' Don Francisco finally admitted.

'Will they be on public display? A woman has her reputation to consider.'

(The Duchess's body would not be easily identified. except perhaps by some of her more intimate friends, but my face could identify me.) That would be unlikely to help my marriage prospects.

Don Francisco looked surprised and amused by what I had said. 'They are not for public display, have no fears.'

'All the same, I wish to meet Don Manuel Godoy,' I said. 'If he is to have my face, I will see his face.'

I had met many of the grandees in the Duchess's circle, but she had not introduced me to Don Manuel Godoy. When I reflected on this, I was sure that she had deliberately kept me from meeting him. She may have felt sorry for me, but that did not mean that she was going to share everything she had.

'As you wish,' Don Francisco said. 'I shall introduce you to Don Manuel. It is only fair, I suppose.'

The Duchess was getting weaker daily, and it was as much as she could do to leave her bed and lie on her satin couch. I sat beside her. Sometimes I read to her. She loved poetry and she said she liked to hear it in my Andulusian accent. She lay there looking over at me with her tired eyes – no longer jealous, no longer haughty. She taught me many things: how to speak more grammatically, all the table etiquette, how to engage important men in conversation, how to comport myself at concerts, at the theatre and at other social events.

I was a quick and willing student, and when Don Francisco took me to meet Don Manuel Godoy, I considered myself as refined and as charming as any highborn Spanish lady. I had taken care to find out as much as I could about Don Manuel before that meeting. He intrigued me, not only because of his position as Prince of Peace and head of the government, but because he had not been born into power. I like that in anyone. He knew how to use his talent, his good looks, he knew how to influence the right people. The King and Queen Maria Luisa are in his pocket; the latter moreover, they say, has taken him to her bed. He married into the aristocracy, just as I intended to do. He was, in fact, a man after my own heart.

Don Francisco was engaged in making a portrait of the Generalissimo to commemorate his victory over the Portuguese in the War of the Oranges. One day he took me with him to Don Manuel's palace. He was waiting in his salon, with his sword and flag by his side, ready for the portrait sitting.

Don Francisco called out from the doorway,

'Don Manuel, may I introduce you to Doña Dolores Martinez?'

Don Manuel strode over to me as if he had been expecting me, took my hand and kissed it, all the time sizing me up. I kept my gaze direct and did not drop my eyes like an embarrassed virgin.

He looked most splendid: tall, with a high forehead, closely cut black hair, and bright appraising eyes. He was wearing yellow breeches and high shining black boots up over his knees. His black jacket was heavily encrusted with gold braid and his scarlet lapels were also edged with gold. He was every inch a conquering hero. I was enslaved.

'I have agreed to let my face be used for your *maja* paintings,' I said as calm as anything, as if I was used to speaking to important people all my life.

Don Manuel smiled and said, 'Well, I am glad to hear that. Indeed, you remind me of – '

Before he could finish, Don Francisco announced that he did not have time to waste, dismissed me, and had Don Manuel assume his hero's pose immediately. I waited in the garden, and when the sitting was over and the two men came out, I knew by the look in Don Manuel's eyes that we would meet again.

About a week later, I received a message saying that he would send his carriage for me to take me to his palace. We became lovers that afternoon. Don Manuel became besotted at once, swore that he would do anything for me, give me anything I asked for. He seemed intrigued by my lack of feminine modesty.

'We both know what we want,' I said, 'so what is the point of wasting time? I do have a price, however. You are married and, no doubt, have many other young women queuing to get into your bed. That does not concern me in the least. I do not fool myself that because we are lovers, my life will be secure or happy. Just as you need honours and power, Don Manuel, I need security, and security means that I find a wealthy husband. He should appreciate my qualities and allow me to live my life without too many restrictions. My price is that you find me such a man.'

Don Manuel laughed and laughed at this. 'I have never met a woman like you,' he said. 'It is a pity indeed that you were not born a man. You would make a formidable opponent on any battlefield. A woman as young as you, so independent-minded, without the slightest pretence at modesty – truly, you are a marvel.'

'I am almost twenty years old,' I retorted. 'I left my youth behind me many years ago.'

I would not tell him anything about my background, I just let him wonder about me. Mystery is a great enchantress. And he was enchanted. He sent his carriage for me so often that the Duchess, who had finished with him by then, warned me that I had better be careful not to attract the attention of the Queen.

'I'm in trouble with the Queen because of you,' Don Manuel told me one afternoon after we had made love. 'She is getting impatient to see me. I have had to buy her a present to mollify her. You will see him in the paddock as you leave. He is called Marcial and he cost me a fortune.'

'And what about mollifying me?' I asked. 'What about my price?'

'Do not worry, my little commander, I have been working on that. I think I may have a suitable man in sight. Don Martin Valdes y Alcazar, a widower with three young children, who has extensive estates in Andalusia.'

And so it was arranged. Don Martin approved of me, and I of him. When I told the Duchess that I had succeeded in my ambition, omitting, of course, the detail of how this had been accomplished, she settled even more money on me; *to give you some more independence.* This was the same woman who once had tried not to pay me thirty reales!

Although I was somewhat preoccupied in my changed circumstances, still I noticed how dramatically the Duchess's health had deteriorated. She suffered from constant headaches, could not sleep and hardly ate a morsel. Her doctors came and went, shaking their heads, and she grew weaker every day. I stayed by her bedside night and day, not only because she seemed to find my presence calming, but because I wanted to be with her. Don Francisco came very often, and when he was with her I left the room. He stayed for hours at a time and left with his head bowed and his walk slow and unsteady, as if he, too, were weak and ill. He suddenly began to look like the really old man he was.

'Ah, Dolores,' he would say to me, 'it does not look good. You must do what you can to make her comfortable.'

And he would shuffle away, sighing and muttering to himself.

They really do love each other, I thought. *The beautiful Duchess and the old painter.*

'Don Manuel wanted me to use his mistress Pepita Tudó's face but as Her Excellency requested me to paint yours, it is as she wished,' Don Francisco told me one day before he started on the work.

I would lie on her couch in the same position as the Duchess had, and he would work as silently, but much more slowly, than he had in Sanlúcar. My face looks fine on the Duchess's body. We are, after all, not unalike.

Her Excellency had hardly enough strength to raise herself on her elbow to see the paintings when Don Francisco finally had them brought into her bedroom more than a year after they had been finished.

'You have done a good job, Francisco, even if you have flattered me a little here and there,' she said with a weak smile. 'Velasquez would be proud of such paintings. And he has caught your expression very well, hasn't he, Dolores?'

These were almost the last words the Duchess spoke. That night her breathing seemed to be laboured and her pulse very weak, so I sent at once for her doctors. By the time they arrived with their useless medicines, Her Excellency had become unconscious. She remained like that for two dreadful days. Her sister-in-law, the Marquise of Villafranca, came to be at my dear Duchess's bedside and members of the household also gathered in her bedroom, all of us helpless and distraught. Poor little Maria de la Luz especially was inconsolable and would not move from the Duchess's bed, where she lay with her arms around her adopted mother's neck.

On the third morning, 5 July 1802, the Duchess of Alba died surrounded by her family, among whom were Maria de la Luz, Luisito, Benito the old monk, Trinidad the old black woman, another of her protégés, Don Francisco and me. He had arrived ten minutes before and was holding her hand as she took her last light breath. I have never seen a man more distraught with grief. He left the palace at once and was seen wandering the streets of Madrid like an old tramp long after midnight.

9

ANDALUSIA, 1803

What an almighty fuss followed the Duchess's death! Godoy and the Queen, and God knows who else, disputing and trying to overturn her will (in which she had left most of her wealth to her adopted family), and taking her treasures. The Queen was seen soon afterwards wearing the Duchess's diamonds and pearls and Godoy claimed her palace in Madrid. There were rumours that she had been poisoned and certain persons' names were mentioned in that context. My beautiful Duchess had been the subject of so many rumours when she was alive and it was not surprising that her death was yet another subject for scandal. But as regards the poisoning, the Marquise of Villafranca testified that this was not true. Who knows why she died so young and in such mysterious circumstances. Perhaps we will never know.

I attended her funeral with Benito, the lame old monk, and Maria de la Luz and Trinidad, an old black woman whom the Duchess had taken into her care, and all the rest of the strays she had adopted. Don Francisco was with us, looking like death himself. The Duchess of Osuna and her husband were the only nobles I recognised in the small congregation. My Duchess had stipulated that her funeral was to be private, that there should be no eulogies. In total contrast to the flamboyance of her public life, she desired a very private funeral.

I married Don Martin and have settled into my new life back home in Andalusia. I live quite near Sanlúcar. I keep my portfolio of *Los Caprichos* in my bureau and occasionally take it out and look at those magnificent and disturbing prints. They affect me greatly. As did their creator.

When I think of Don Francisco Goya, I think of the sun, full of energy and heat, throwing a blazing light on a dark world, searching out vice and hypocrisy. I think of his other work too; the erotic Sanlúcar album, the naked *maja*. I remember the sadness in his eyes when we talked about dead babies. I remember his many acts of his kindness to the Duchess of Alba at the end of her short life.

Mostly, when I bring him to mind, I see his heavy shoulders bending towards his easel, a paintbrush or a pencil attached to his hand like another finger.

10
ROSARIO
BADRID, 1833

My life is not at all what I had envisaged five years ago after Papa died. Mama and I were not allowed to return to la Quinta del Sordo. It almost broke my heart to know that I would never again walk in his gardens, or see his black wall paintings, or sit under the fig tree where he had told me stories from mythology and the Bible. Never hear again the water in the fountain where the old bull and the young torero had splashed each other after the corrida.

We came to Madrid more or less destitute. If Papa had left us some money in his will, as he had so often promised, we have not been given it. Javier threw one thousand reales at Mama before he ordered us out of our home in Bordeaux. I became a drawing teacher to Queen Isabella. She seemed pleased with my teaching and told me frequently that I was very talented. Papa had often told me the same thing, but what good did that do? I needed more than praise. I needed practice. I needed commissions. I needed a patron.

Her Majesty seemed very interested in me for some reason.

'You are a very pretty young woman Rosario,' she said
when I had been teaching her for a few weeks. 'You must have
many suitors.'

'No, Your Majesty,' I replied. And I left it at that. Suitors
require women with dowries.

'Weiss, that is a German name, is it not?' she asked next
as she was focussing on a still life of flowers in a blue jug. 'Is
your father German?'

'My father is dead.' How I hated being asked questions
about either of my parents.

The Queen looked at my face and asked no more
questions. I can be as stubborn as he was. One might
have thought it would have been in my interest to have
courted favour with her so that she might have secured me
commissions from grandees at court, but, as I am a woman,
I considered that I was unlikely to receive commissions from
them for portraits or to decorate their chapels. If I could have
used my father's name, however, I often wondered if that
would have helped. I was in danger of becoming quite bitter
in those early years as I struggled to support my mother and
myself and I saw no opportunity of becoming what my father
had desired for me... an independent artist. I had no time
to develop my talent and no money to study the great art in
Italy and France.

Her Majesty continued working on her composition
for another ten minutes. 'Your accent sounds a trifle foreign,
Rosario. Did you grow up in France?'

'I was born in Spain, and spent four years of my life in
Bordeaux. I learned French at school there, and maybe that
is why my accent sounds foreign. I was ten years old when
we went to live in France and fourteen when we left. Those
years, I have heard, are very formative,' I said in a rush, as if by

giving a lot of information at once, I might discourage further questioning about my past.

'Where did you learn to be an artist?' Queen Isabella asked me a few weeks later. 'I believe that you are an accomplished miniaturist, as well as being an expert at making lithographs.'

Where had she discovered that information? Did she know more about me than she pretended?

'I studied drawing at the atelier of a Monsieur Lacôme, and the technique of making miniatures with a Monsieur Vernet in Bordeaux, but my father taught me most of what I know about art. He worked on miniatures and lithographs towards the end of his life, and he allowed me to help him.'

I did not tell Her Majesty that my father believed that I possessed special qualities. I did not tell her what he had written in a letter to his friend Don Martin Ferrer:

The amazing child wishes to learn to do miniatures and I wish it as well, for to do at her age what she has done is the most phenomenal thing in the world.

I did not speak of these things, not because I did not believe that what my father said might well be true, and not because I thought it would be boastful, but because I did not want to encourage any questions as to my father's identity. Javier and Mariano had forbidden me ever to claim him and until I have proved to myself that I deserved to use his name, as he instructed me, I preferred to remain as anonymous as possible.

'He taught you well,' Her Majesty said. 'I, too, would like to learn how to make miniatures, so we shall continue with that, when you think my drawing is sufficiently good.'

'Thank you, Your Majesty. I would be most honoured to teach you all I know.'

Her Majesty appointed me to a permanent position as her drawing mistress. She also obtained a reasonably well-paid job for me as a copyist at the Prado. I liked her well enough. She was not patronising and did not treat me as if I was a servant. Although I was grateful for the stipend I received for my lessons and I enjoyed my copyist job in the Prado, as it gave me an opportunity to learn lessons from the great masters such as Velasquez and my father's other favourite painter, Rembrandt, I regretted that I did not have enough time to devote to practising my own art, to following my own imagination. I told myself, however, that I must be patient, that I could not fulfil my father's last command just yet.

Still, I had to confess that I found it hard to be patient, living with Mama in our stuffy little attic room in an alley off Calle Valverde. She complained so much about everyone and everything; Papa, Javier, Mariano, Gumersinda, our lack of money and position, the plain food we had to eat, *everything*.

I often lay in bed, staring at the ceiling, remembering Papa's last words to me:

One day you will be a great painter, my daughter. Always make art from your own imagination... Be independent as an artist... Swear to me that nobody will dictate what art you will make.

When will that be? I wondered. A copyist does nothing original, and a drawing mistress makes nothing new, either. Did Papa forget that I am female? Which women have become great artists? Artemisia Gentileschi is the only one I can think of, and she had the good fortune to be her father's, Orazio, only child, so that he taught her everything and gave her commissions. Papa never sent me to Paris to study, as he once promised. But perhaps he considered me too young at fourteen to go there. Had he lived, I am sure he would have sent me or even taken me there with him. He really loved me. And he believed in me. I must always keep that in my heart.

As time went on and I feared that I would never become a real artist, I reconsidered my earlier reluctance to curry favour with Her Majesty. As she seemed to like me and respect my work, I began to hope that she might help me to find enlightened patrons who would allow me to use my own imagination. So that eventually I could be the artist Papa wished me to become. Then I could use his name. That time has yet to come, but I am more hopeful now than I have ever been of fulfilling his wishes for me.

As I was lying in my bed one evening, exhausted after my lessons and my work at the Prado, my mother flounced into the room.

'There you are, you lazy girl, daydreaming again. How are we to eat better if you spend your time lying in bed, instead of making pictures to sell?'

A flame of anger flared in me. My mother was so unfair, so endlessly demanding.

'Mama, you have no right to speak to me like that,' I said, trying not to cry in frustration. 'You know full well how hard and long I work at the Palace and at the Prado. What more can I do? Why don't *you* find work, if you are not satisfied with the money I earn?'

My mother ignored the last remark. She has always disregarded what she does not wish to hear or to know.

'We've been back in Madrid for almost five years now, Rosario, and we're still as poor as beggars. You were so full of yourself when we arrived, assuring me that your inventive art would make us a fortune, as your father's had for him. What happened to that great vision, Rosario?'

'Why must you be so unfair, so unrealistic, Mama? I was fourteen years old then and I thought that life was full of possibilities if one had talent. I know better now. It takes more than talent to succeed. Papa was a man, first of all, and you should not need reminding that it is much easier for a man to make his own way in this world than it is for a woman. Secondly, how old was Papa before he was successful? Before his art brought him wealth? He was twenty-five years old when he got his first commission, and over forty before he was successful. It took that long. I am nineteen and a woman. Thirdly, you may have noticed that, unlike Papa, I have no wealthy or influential friends to promote my interests, nobody to obtain commissions for me. And, frankly, your behaviour is unlikely to draw such people to me; always running around town complaining endlessly about our situation, about Gumersinda and Javier and Mariano. There is no dignity in that, Mama; it serves no purpose. What is done is done, and that's an end to it. I earn enough to pay the rent and to feed us. I'm sorry we have little left over for new clothes for you. I regret you cannot have a fancy new comb every week. We survive – why can't that be enough for you?'

As I spoke, I knew there was little point reasoning with my mother, that in another few days she would be at it again, complaining. I looked at her eternally disappointed and disapproving expression, and I saw that resentment and bitterness, like vinegar left too long in a bowl, had pitted her once beautiful face, had made it almost ugly. I felt pity for her.

And pity for myself too. Why could I not be like other young women of my age, going to balls, or even walking with friends in the evening along the Prado, where I might laugh and enjoy myself, and perhaps meet a handsome suitor who would recognise my talent and overlook the fact that I have no dowry? Nineteen was not that old, and yet I lived the life of an old maid, working all day, responsible for my mother, and unable to develop artistically. If only Papa had… if only he had… but I stopped myself thinking into that hole. It yielded nothing; better to concentrate for the present on making a friend of the Queen.

'You said your father made miniatures towards the end of his life. When did he die?' Her Majesty asked casually while I was getting ready the copper plate on which we would make our first engraving. I took that as a good sign that she wanted to know me better. I considered that she was not simply being polite.

'Five years ago.'

'And he is buried in his family vault in Spain?'

She had already winkled out of me the fact that he was not French.

'No, his tomb is in France.'

Queen Isabella tried to suppress an exasperated sigh. I imagined that she was thinking that attempting to prise information from me was like watching wine trickle from the tiniest pinprick in a *bota*. So, remembering my plan to engender her goodwill and support, I punctured the *bota* a little more.

'Papa was eighty-two when he died. He was a great artist and produced many different genres of art – cartoons for tapestries, portraits, frescoes, lithographs, engravings, as well as miniatures.'

'Such a talented and prolific artist must have been well known. Five years dead, you say? Not so long ago. Yet I cannot recall an artist by that name,' said Her Majesty, shaking her head a little. 'Weiss? Weiss? No… nobody of that name. You told me that your Papa was Spanish. Where exactly did he come from?'

'From Aragon, from a little village near Saragossa, I believe. I have never been there.'

'Surely you go to visit your Papa's relatives – your uncles and aunts, your cousins?'

'Papa was sixty-eight when I was born, and so his parents and brothers and sisters are all dead now. If I have any cousins in Saragossa, I do not know them.'

We had just finished making her Majesty's first engraving. It had turned out quite well and the Queen was delighted.

'I know,' she said, 'that the skill and finish in the piece is mostly your work, but it is my first attempt and it is quite good, don't you think? This calls for a celebration.' And she ordered a bottle of the finest wine to be brought to us. 'We shall drink to the Queen's artistic success.'

She handed me a crystal glass of red wine. We drank a toast together, and then another. I felt relaxed, appreciated and grateful, and perhaps that was why I found myself being more open than I have ever been in the Queen's presence.

'Your father was obviously a very good teacher,' she said with a confidence-inviting smile. 'Tell me more about him. As an artist, I mean,' she added hastily, seeing the openness about to close in my eyes. Really, if the King or her courtiers could have seen her, practically *begging* me to speak to her!

'Papa was a genius. He could paint and draw any subject. He never stopped working. At eighty years of age he was painting for ten hours a day without stopping, and often worked late into the night too, especially when he was doing his own work.'

'What do you mean by *his own work*?'

'I mean the work he wanted to do for himself. When I was a child, for example, he spent months painting the walls of our house at La Quinta – with pictures of course. And when we were living in Bordeaux, he worked for ages on a series of miniatures on ivory, which he made for himself, not for any patron.'

'And what was the subject of these works which he did for himself?'

'There was not one subject – the works were not landscapes or portraits. They were fantasies, I suppose – that is the most accurate term – made from his imagination, as well as satires and ironic observations of human behaviour.' The wine had loosened my tongue, but, though I spoke more freely than I had ever done, I still did not utter my father's name.

'I asked him once to explain the meaning of his work. He put down his brushes and said quite crossly: 'If I have to *tell* you the meaning, child, why should I go to all the trouble of putting paint on canvas or on walls? Why should I spend days and weeks scraping etchings, inhaling acid and lead? The meaning is *in* my work. Use your eyes, child. Look. Look. *Just look!*'

'He sounds like a wise man, your father. But maybe he expected too much of the viewers. Which painters did he admire?'

'Papa told me that he had three masters: Nature, Rembrandt, and Velázquez. Those miniatures I spoke about just now – he said they were original in the method of their execution, because they were done in stipple and resembled the brushwork of Velázquez. Some of his portraits – though not, of course, in any way copying Rembrandt – show his influence. I mean Papa, like Rembrandt, was also interested in the character of his sitter, and I do not think he ever flattered anyone. He also painted many self-portraits, like Rembrandt.

As for his other master – Nature. He told me once: 'Nature has claws. They fool themselves who see only light and surface beauty. The noble lion rips open the throat of its prey. Why should we imagine that we humans are any different?' Another day he said: 'The spores of decay are already at work in the newly blooming rosebud and in the bones of the most beautiful young girl.' I think he meant that if we ignore the claws of destruction and the spores of decay, we deceive ourselves, but if we are aware of the dark behind the light, and of the potential claw behind the smile, we shall not be deceived.'

I stopped suddenly. I had spoken too long and I was afraid that Her Majesty might form a negative view of my father, and I was also aware that I might have given away too much about him. How many artists have produced such scathing comments on human nature as my father in *Los Caprichos*? Her Majesty might guess who he was. She might well have seen the prints. I had been told that many grandees bought sets, including the Duchess of Osuna.

'Your father sounds a most intriguing and original man. I should like to hear more about him. Another time perhaps. Our lesson is finished for today. We shall meet again next week,' Her Majesty finished her wine and the conversation. I was much relieved.

Back in the claustrophobic attic that evening I tried to practise making portraits. Portraits might be the gateway into becoming a respected artist. Papa, after all, had made most of his wealth from his portraits of grandees. I asked my mother to model for me.

'Would you sit still, Mama, please? How can I draw you if you keep fidgeting like that? I have to practise doing portraits if I am to find patrons. Portraits are what they want.'

Mama sniffed impatiently, but stopped shifting about in her chair: 'I suppose I can't talk either.'

'It's hard for me to concentrate if you do. Papa could not tolerate conversation while he was working, and now I know why.'

'Papa, Papa, always Papa. When are you going to forget Papa?' she barked. 'Papa did not remember you, did he? Or me. His word meant nothing. After all my years of devoted care of him! The things I had to put up with, the sacrifices I made.'

'Mama, stop it! Stop it at once. I can't bear to hear you going over and over all that again. I am sure he meant to keep his promise to us, but then he became paralysed and was unable to sign a new will. He expected Javier to carry out his wishes. And *do not* start in on Javier now. We have been over that ground too. How can I concentrate on drawing when you stir me up so much?'

My mother was about to open her mouth again. I could not continue. I threw down my pastels. 'Oh, will there never be an end to all this? It is intolerable.' I cried and I despised the break in my voice.

'How like your father you are, so irritable if I merely open my mouth.' she said and flounced out of the room.

'I am very interested in what you told me about your father's theories of art,' the Queen said at our next lesson. 'Tell me more.'

I had no trouble remembering word for word what Papa told me and so I was happy to oblige.

'Papa said that there is no colour or line in nature; that only sun and shadow exist. He said that there are bodies, I think he meant forms, which are illuminated and those which are not. There are planes that advance, and those that recede – relief and depth. Papa also said that he did not perceive line or detail. He did not count the hairs in the beard of a man passing by, for instance, nor the buttons on a frock coat. When he was working, he always stood a good distance from his subject and painted the mass, not the detail. One of his favourite sayings was: *My brush cannot be expected to see better than me.*

No colour or line. Planes that advance and planes that recede. Illuminated and non-illuminated forms, the Queen wrote carefully in her little gold-leaf notebook, 'Very interesting, my dear. *The mass and not the detail.* And I spend so much of my time and effort trying to observe and depict every little detail. Perhaps that is why the things I draw seem so dead.'

'Your Majesty is making a lot of progress,' I assured her. 'Drawing is not easy. It takes years of practice to see things properly, to co-ordinate the hand and eye.'

At that moment I felt strangely old and experienced.

The next moment the tables turned again. 'Isn't it time you thought about a husband, Rosario? Is your mother arranging a match for you?'

'I have not thought of marriage.' Then in a rush of confidence, I continued: 'I cannot. First I want to become an independent artist, working from my own imagination. I do not mean,' I added hastily lest Her Majesty should think me ungrateful, 'that I do not also want to do other work.'

'But your mother, does she not wish to see you successfully married?'

'I am sure that would please her greatly.'

There was nothing that my mother would have liked better than to have me married off to some rich man who would keep both mother and daughter in style. But there was no dowry, and there was the paternity problem. So what was the point of thinking of marriage? Besides, I certainly did not want to be married off to anyone, however rich. I wanted to choose my own husband.

When I felt desperate, trapped, I had a fantasy of becoming a *maja* and snaring a handsome and rich young noble as my lover. Why not wear a mantilla, and a black silk skirt and play a tambourine and flirt behind an ivory fan and carry a poniard in my garter and have a *majo* protector, who wears a cape and smokes black cigars? Why not have some fun? To hell with copying all day in the Prado. To hell with teaching drawing to a woman without much talent. But I did not, could not, indulge in that fantasy, as I would be compromised. I would never become the artist I had promised Papa.

'I am interested in what you tell me your father said about his own invention,' the Queen continued presently. 'What did he mean by that? Surely an artist copies what he sees and does not invent?'

'Papa meant that the artist selects and arranges and makes what he sees his own, so that he is not a servile copyist. I mean a great artist, of course, not someone like me. I have to learn by copying and practising,' I said quickly, remembering my place, as well as my father's sermons on the inventive imagination.

Weeks passed without further interrogation. We concentrated on making pictures and forgot while we worked the difference in our status. I began to feel more and more at ease in Her Majesty's company and I believed Queen Isabella trusted my integrity as she confided in me what she could not tell her husband, or advisors, or indeed anyone in her family. Art is a leveller, I concluded. That is its power. It strips privilege to common humanity. In order to see beyond the veneer, however, we have to practise it, or failing that, to appreciate art for what it is. That is why my father was not impressed by power or status. That is why he could show us humans the world as it really is and what we really are, in all its and our positive and negative aspects. There is darkness as well as light and sometimes the dark obliterates the light. In his life he saw too much darkness in the state of our country – the wars, the cruelty, the vanities and corruption of the wealthy and powerful, the poverty and suffering as well as the superstitions of the masses. His deafness, he told me once, allowed him to see better.

Her Majesty offered to have her dressmaker make some new dresses for me. She gave me gifts of beautiful fans, combs and fine shawls, some of which my mother appropriated saying that I had little need of such fine things. Her Majesty seemed a bit unsure as to how she might give me these things, as if she were afraid of offending my pride. However, I took them as a sign of her increasing affection for me and of the possibility of her assisting me in obtaining commissions. My mother was not in the least grateful, in fact she was mad with jealousy. 'You'll soon be calling the Queen *mother*,' she said, her mouth twisted in a sneer. In truth, there is no pleasing that woman. I feel my store of pity for her is limited. *Yet, she is my mother*, I tell myself, *and she has endured much since Papa died.*

'We shall not draw today, my dear. It is so pleasant outside, let us stroll in the garden and have a nice conversation instead,' Her Majesty said one afternoon in April when a breeze moved the curtains, and the scent of mimosa drifted through the open windows. As we walked together in the Palace garden, I realised that I could not hold out any longer. She wanted to know the story of my life, so I finally began to tell her almost everything she wished to know: about my idyllic life at La Quinta del Sordo, about my young and beautiful mother (as she was then) living with my much older father. I supplied some censored details about our move to France. I told her about my studies there and about all the time I spent watching my father work and learning from him. I did not mention my half-brother or his family, and I said nothing much else about my father, except some more of his theories of art. The Queen listened attentively to everything I said, but it was clear that she still wanted to know the full story of my father. I do not understand fully why I was so reluctant to reveal his identity. I somehow felt that if he had chosen not to openly claim me as his daughter, why should I openly claim him as my father?

'And this mysterious Aragonese father of yours, what about him? How did he come to have a German name? And if he was a genius, as you say, how is it I have never heard of him?' The Queen asked gently, taking my arm.

I could evade no longer. 'His name was not Weiss. That was the name of my mother's husband.'

Her Majesty looked puzzled.

'My mother's husband was not my father. She was separated from him before I was born.'

'Who, then, was your father?' she asked and she took my hand in hers and held it as one would a hurt child's.

'He was the man my mother went to live with, first as his housekeeper and then as his companion. Mama says that theirs was not a conventional marriage because she was still legally married to Señor Weiss, and that society is strange, in that a woman's children are always counted as belonging to her legal husband, whether that is the case or not.'

'Your real father's name?'

I could no longer deny him. 'Don Francisco de Goya was my father's name.'

I felt a great sense of relief that I had claimed Papa at last and to the highest personage in the land. I knew there was no going back now and Javier and Mariano could rage all they liked. Queen Isabella struggled not to show how stunned she was by this revelation.

'My dear Rosario, you should use his name! One of Spain's brightest stars! What doors that would open for you, my dear! Why do you not?'

'Because, first of all, I promised Papa that I would use his name only when I was a good enough artist and I am far from achieving that. And there are other reasons ...'

'Yes? Other reasons?'

'Javier, my father's son, my half-brother, and Mariano, his grandson, and Gumersinda, who is his daughter-in-law, have forbidden me to use the Goya name. Besides, I have no official proof that he was my father. He informally adopted me when I was seven, and said I should be treated like his daughter, but he did not actually ever declare publicly that I was his daughter. That is why I do not use his name.'

We ended the walk and our conversation there. My feelings as I walked home were very mixed. What would Her Majesty think of my father? I did not want her to have a bad opinion of him for any reason. Papa was a generous and kind man. He loved me. He must have his own reasons for not claiming me publicly as his daughter.

'Don Francisco de Goya died a wealthy man,' Her Majesty said before we started our next lesson. 'From the royal records I have discovered how much he charged for each painting and also how much he had earned as salary during many years as Chief Court Painter. On top of that, there the income he had from his numerous wealthy patrons. Yet you, his only daughter, my dear Rosario, are not well off and you have to make your own living. Why is that?'

'I do not wish to displease your Majesty, but I would prefer not to discuss that matter. My father was good and kind. Not everyone is. He is not responsible for my present situation,' I said and my voice was shaking.

'I see,' said her majesty, looking as if she did not see at all. But she was discrete and questioned me no further.

'We would like you to come to a ball which will take place here next week,' Queen Isabella said to me at the end of our lesson some weeks later as I was putting on my shawl to leave. 'I have a very handsome young man in mind as your escort.'

I was very pleased at first and blushed to think I might meet a handsome young man, but ... 'Thank you for the invitation, Your Majesty,' I said in a low voice, 'I regret I cannot accept it.'

'Why ever not? You are young, Rosario. You must enjoy yourself!'

I could think of nothing to say except the truth. 'Because I have no dress fine enough for a ball... or shoes... or anything.'

'Your father gave everything to Javier and his family, is that right?'

'Well, yes. They own everything.' The admission pained me more than I can say.

'And they have not given you a share of your father's wealth? Your half-brother has given you and your mother nothing?'

'Javier does not recognise me as his half-sister.'

I felt the long dammed flood gates open and a gush of bitterness emerged. 'When he ordered us to leave our home in Bordeaux, we hardly had time to pack our clothes. Gumersinda even tried to take *The Maid of Bordeaux* from us – that's what Papa called his last painting, which he did of me, and which he had *given* to Mama. And Mariano roared at me as soon as we got back from Papa's funeral: 'I know what you've been scheming, you little bastard ... Oh, I beg your pardon, Your Majesty.'

'Do not worry, my dear, I've heard that word before. Go on – what else did Mariano say?'

'He said: 'Don't think you or your mother will ever see La Quinta again. Don't think I don't know you've been whispering about it to my grandfather, but it's mine now, and you'll never live there again. Never!'

'You poor, poor girl,' the Queen said, patting my hand repeatedly and looked at me with such sympathy. 'You've been disgracefully cheated.'

'My mother lived sixteen years with Papa. She looked after him like a wife when he was old and ill. And that brat Mariano dared to call her names! Papa loved me, he always treated me as his daughter, and Mariano called me a bastard!'

My voice broke again but my anger was too strong for tears. I could say no more. After my outburst, I felt as if all my energy and courage, which had sustained me during the five long years of hardship and struggle since Papa's death, had been swept away in the flood of words. I regretted having told the Queen my story, and feared that now the dam had burst, I might become as bitter as my mother.

Her Majesty was full of sympathy and concern. She sent me a beautiful ball gown, shoes, combs and fans together with an invitation to the Palace ball.

'Don José Fernandez will escort you,' she wrote. 'I have told him a little about you and he is intrigued by your artistic talents. He is a kind young man and heir to a large estate in Aragon. He will appreciate your worth, I am sure. And we can arrange terms, if you find him suitable.'

Mama was gleeful at the prospect of a rich young suitor for me. As I was afraid to go against the Queen's wishes, I dressed reluctantly for the ball. What could I say to this Don José? What had Her Majesty told him about me, about my father?

Mama noticed my reluctance and admonished me. 'Now is your chance to obtain a better life for us, girl. For pity's sake, don't spoil this opportunity by talking about being an independent artist. Just say whatever this Don José wishes to hear. I cannot live in this garret a month longer. Now get some colour in those cheeks of yours, and try not to look so miserable.'

Disillusionment seeped like slow poison through my veins. If I was to be married off, how could I fulfil my father's expectations of me? *Caprice and invention.* It was all very well for him to speak of independence. Had he sincerely wished me to be a true artist, why did he not ensure that I could live independently so that I could create my own art and one day use his name with pride? He did not mean to be cruel, I consoled myself. Gumersinda was the one who had caused our poverty. But it is also true that Papa could not cross Javier and Mariano, even to protect and to claim his only daughter. He who seemed so strong, so stubborn, was also weak.

To please the Queen and my mother, I attended the ball with Don José. I did not attempt to be other than what I am. He seemed to be intrigued by me. Goodness knows what Her Majesty had told him. When we started to speak about art he exclaimed: 'In my opinion, Don Francisco Goya is the most honest and the best Spanish painter we have ever had.'

'Why do you think that? The most honest?'

'Because he was not afraid to deal with the darkness in all our souls. Because he was a realist. He made art to disturb us, to make us think about our society, about the human condition.'

'How do you know his work?'

'Well, apart from the fact that anyone who is interested in art in this country must know him, he was our Court Painter after all, and produced such marvellous work, I am from Aragon, like he was. From Saragossa. My family knew his wife's family. Not very well, it is true, but enough to know what good and honest people the Bayeaus were. Do you know his work?' he asked, with such a look of warmth and interest in his kind brown eyes.

So the Queen had not told him who I was. That was respectful of her. I will tell him myself when I consider it is appropriate.

'I know it very well indeed. Don Francisco Goya was a genius. His art will not be fully understood perhaps for generations. He was before his time. Like a prophet.'

Once started, I spoke at length about Papa's work, about his tapestry cartoons, his many portraits, the black paintings in La Quinta, *Los Caprichos,* the enormous Second of May painting, his *Tauromaquia* etchings of the history of bullfighting and his miniatures on ivory. I could have continued for hours but stopped myself. I feared that I had already given away too much. However, Don José paid rapt attention to everything I said.

'I can see that you are truly a great admirer of Don Francisco Goya,' he said finally with a look of admiration and respect in his eyes.' You know more about his art than anyone I have ever met. Of course, that may be because, according to Her Majesty, you are a very talented artist. She told me that you are most interested in working freely, from your own imagination. *Caprice and invention*, I believe were the words she used.'

Don José is a most charming man. We married last June. He has set up a studio for me in our house. I am practising hard to become the artist Papa expected me to be and I am having some success. It will take time. It took Papa years. My husband supports me in every way. He is proud of me. We have bought Mama a house in Madrid. Saragossa is too provincial for her, she says, and I am glad of that. I have peace to get on with my work here.

When I go into Saragossa with my husband we sometimes pass the house where Papa and his wife Doña Josefa lived when he was beginning his great career. I have visited the church of El Pilar, about which he spoke as he lay dying, to see the frescoes he created there and once more I am full of wonder at how versatile my Papa was; so many frescoes, portraits, engravings, miniatures. Such energy, such passion!

This amazing man, this genius artist, Francisco de Goya was my Papa who bought me beautiful red shoes when we lived in La Quinta, who hid ribbons and spinning tops under leaves for me and pieces of chocolate behind the green water pitcher in the kitchen. This devoted father was also the artist of the dark, the celebrator of beauty, of the innocence of children, the harsh critic of society, the relentless pursuer of the unpalatable truths ever lurking behind the facade.

When I think of my dear Papa, I hear once more his voice from long ago when I was a child – seeking to explain himself, to explain all of us, and perhaps also seeking compassion.

This world is a masquerade, Mariquita; face, clothing, voice – everything is meant to deceive. Everyone wants to appear what he is not, each deluding the other and not even knowing himself.

ACKNOWLEDGEMENTS

My thanks to David Carrión, Dr. Philip Deacon, Professor David T. Gies, Marie Heaney, Emily Lane, Jonathan Williams, Síne Quinn, Maria Tirelli and Svetlana Pironko.

ABOUT THE AUTHOR

Fionnuala Brennan started writing ghost stories at the age of seven and has been writing ever since: journals, accounts of her travels in Europe, Africa and Asia, short stories. Eventually, when she had finished rearing her two daughters and working full time, she decided to release some of this stuff from captivity in her desk drawer and published *On a Greek Island*, a travel memoir, a novel called *All Things Return,* several prize-winning short stories as well as a two-act play *Bloodroot*.

The Painter's Women results from her fascination with Francisco de Goya.

To learn more about Fionnuala Brennan please visit *www. betimesbooks.com.*

Made in the USA
Charleston, SC
26 September 2015